The Traveler
Ken Page and the
Fallen Angel

The Traveler Series
An Adventure Story

Daniel L. Rogers
Mary Darragh Page

Clear Light Arts – Texas USA

The Traveler Ken Page and the Fallen Angel

Graphic design and electronic production by Alan Klemp

First Published in 1995 by:

Ken Page *Heart & Soul Healing*Clear Light Arts
Institute of Multidimensional Cellular Healing
www.KenPage.com   1-800-809-1290 - US
276 Watauga Village Dr., Suite H. PMB 222
Boone, N.C. USA 28607

ISBN 0-9649703-0-9

Acknowledgements

The author's wish to express their appreciation to the following: to Nita Page, whose love, support and encouragement made this novel possible, to Diane Cooper, for her editorial insight, and to the entire staff and amazing people at Kismet Cafe, San Marcos, Texas.

And most of all, we would like to thank Ken Page and Polarity (aka Rascals).

Introduction

In 1959, I had the chance to see a famous Tarot card reader, whom a friend of mine offered to pay for if I would go along for the adventure. My friend told me this Tarot card reader had predicted the course of her life and she wanted to see what the fortune teller would say about me. I submitted to the experience, providing the woman with the date, time, and place of my birth, and nothing else. My friend knew nothing about my past, so she couldn't have told the woman anything about me. I expected to hear a lot of oft quoted generalities and a few things that might be accidentally right on. But what I heard instead, was a detailed account of my life, as it had been up to that moment, down to the subject matter of the novels I had tried and failed to write. She even told me the names of the characters in my novels and how writing, and not teaching acting, was what I most wanted to do although I would do both all my life. She said I would never make any money, but not to be concerned for at the last instant someone would come along to give me what I needed. Then she started to relate to me what would happen in the next thirty or so years. She said I would have two heart attacks when I was fifty years of age which I thought sounded strange. I thought Tarot card readers weren't suppose to tell you the really scary stuff, but the woman made clear to me that I was a special case, and that my heart problem would be the incident that would lead me to what my life, on this planet, was really about. I always doubted those who knew what anything was 'really about', especially something as complicated and maze-like as a life.

She said that at the age of fifty I would leave my second wife and then meet a person who would change my life. I asked her how I would know this person, and she said a very odd thing that I was to never forget. "He will tell you that he was holding your hand, standing at the foot of the cross at Calvary."

After that reading I dismissed all Tarot card readers and never saw one again. I went on to be a writer and an acting teacher. When I was fifty years of age I had a near fatal heart condition and subsequent surgery. After a year of slow convalescence I moved to Wimberley, Texas, at the invitation of Ken Page who was married to my second ex-wife, Mary Darragh Page. Ken told me this story, even before he said hello. He had just picked me up at the airport, when he had the oddest vision. He saw himself standing beside me at the foot of the cross when Jesus died. "That sounds really funny, doesn't it?" I did not laugh.

What you are about to read is the story of what happened after that. All of the information in this novel concerning the Holy Grail I later verified as being correct, but at the time of the writing neither of the authors had the vaguest idea of the contents of the original epic poem. To our amazement, even the smallest details of the Holy Grail legend, such as references to a ship on which no living person could be seen or to Joseph's son seeing Christ's face as a ball of flaming light, were details of the novel before we found them, again, in the poem. I leave it to my readers to make out of this what they will.

Daniel Rogers
Wimberley, Texas, USA
July 31, 1995

The day I met Ken Page I knew my life had taken a turn. In our time together, I have experienced the intensity and joy of life's journey traveled with a partner, lover and friend. We are on a spiritual adventure together and I will always consider myself extremely blessed that I know and love this man.

Ken was the one who first suggested that Daniel come to live with us in Texas. Although Danny and I had continued to be very good friends after our marriage ended, Ken had never met Daniel and I was astonished that he was willing to offer my ex-husband a home with us. Ken also allowed Daniel and I total artistic freedom in writing this book regardless of the fact that Daniel was very critical of the New Age metaphysical movement. These two examples, along with many others, illustrate to me what a remarkable man I've married. For Ken, the possibilities are endless. His open mindedness and willingness to trust and explore new ideas and ways of being both amaze and delight me.

I have learned that the more aware and attuned to my special journey I become, the deeper the issues are that I am asked to confront and master. Ken and I, as partners, act as mirrors for each other in this process and part of this process has been the acknowledgment and acceptance of my dark side as well as my light side. This is a natural part of the human condition, the human polarity consciousness. My acceptance of every aspect of my humanity has allowed me to work with my most basic issues of survival and control more easily because these issues no longer carry the same charge for me. I choose to embrace my male and female, my angels as well as my darkest muses. I have learned that my path is about accepting all the truth and all the unbelievable magic and discovery of being human.

Mary Darragh Page
Wimberley, Texas

The Traveler
Ken Page and the
Fallen Angel

The Traveler Series
An Adventure Story

"All time is perhaps eternally present."

T. S. Eliot

Prologue

The Legend

Once upon a time, long ago, there was a four year old child. His father said he was four but his mother said he was one thousand, four hundred and sixty days of age and his uncle said he was thirty-five thousand and forty hours of age and his grandfather disagreed with his uncle and said, 'You're all wrong. My grandson is two million, one hundred and two thousand and four hundred minutes of age.'

One day, as the boy was lying on his uncle's bed, a big soft bed, and only pretending to be asleep, he wondered whether it was true that his uncle was really going to take him aboard the ship, like he had promised.

The child remembered everything, remembered being awakened, taken up into his uncles arms and carried out to the car. He remembered the red car's loud engine starting, but he did not remember who was driving, nor did he remember parking the car or getting out of the car. He woke up on the deck of a big boat. At first, a fat faced man said

*the boy wouldn't be allowed on the boat
and his uncle said it had better be
allowed and the fat faced man looked
very angry. And then a skinny faced man
came up and he also said that a four
year old would not be allowed and so
there was a big fight, but eventually the
child was allowed to go aboard. There
would be a lot of time before the boat
went to sea.*

*Everyone seemed very happy until
the great humming noise began. Only
the child started to cry. All the men were
looking around. The air had turned
green. Two men were screaming. Hades
was coming up from the depths of the
sea. And an eternal stretch of black skies
was falling, down from the high vaulted
heavens. The little boy was crying, and
his uncle was shouting, and the fat faced
man was frozen, half on and half off the
boat. The skinny faced man had grabbed
hold of the child and was helping the
child's uncle to throw him to safety.*

*Once upon a time that always was,
there was a child four years of age who
went aboard a ship, and no one could
agree on how much time had passed
before he returned to land. Is it possible
it could have been two thousand years?*

∞ 1 ∞

My name is Daniel. On January fourth, in the year of our Lord, 1983, I was declared disabled. The state of California and the Federal government agreed, but I was disabled in ways that the government didn't know. There is not one instant when the pain mounts up and knocks you over. No, terror comes in small waves taking its time. It is an ocean that fills up with tablespoons of water added each time you take a breath or look at yourself in the mirror or think about what might have happened to you in the past. The bottom line is that I was a corpse waiting to die, wanting more than anything to die and yet afraid to die; and I had been that corpse most of my life.

My first thought was nothing was wrong that couldn't be fixed. Then I thought it could be fixed, if only I did something, but I knew not what to do. I thought it was a feeling, then I knew it was a pain. I thought I was horrified, then I thought it was the horror the body feels when it has been eaten away by cancer and the fear of dying. Then I thought it was nothing at all and that the fear was in my head, not in my chest. I planned to go to the doctor. I didn't go to the doctor. I planned again to go to the doctor, but I was too afraid to go. At last I went and told him I didn't know if I was going to live. He put me in a hospital and kept me there. At first their tests showed nothing conclusive, however the blood tests showed that I was near death.

After a week of further tests, I was told that my heart would require seven hours of surgery. They were going to saw open my rib cage and peel the infected pericardium from my strangled heart. The pericardium is a fluid-filled membrane that acts as a girdle for the heart, and once infected, it becomes the enemy. On the day your own body rises up against you, it begins by departing a wisdom, a warning from long ago that only the body can hear, a story that the body's pain is the beginning, not the end. I couldn't move without losing my breath or becoming dizzy, and there was that ever present pain in my chest. The pain feels like an intense, long lasting heartburn that even Rolaids cannot soothe. The surgeons scheduled the operation, then moved it up twenty four hours, deciding it wasn't safe to wait.

Those last few hours before the operation, I spent with the thought that I was never again in my life going to feel as good as I felt at that particular moment. For the truth was that when I was my sickest, a feeling of satori came over me. I was lying in bed without any pain, never so relaxed in my life, never so blissful. The bed was now perfect. A perfect ceiling light shrouded me in its warmth. My mind had stopped its worrisome jabber. For once, ghosts from my past weren't judging me, telling me that my world was impossible. Part of me was glad there was a good chance I might never wake up from the operation, that I would expire in a deep and painless sleep.

When I first opened my eyes after seven hours of surgery, I couldn't figure out where I was. Then the terror of knowing that I was still alive began. Not only was I still alive but the real hell, the all-out war with endurance, was now awaiting me. The room I was in appeared to have walls covered with dirt and blood. A reddish brown tint hung in the air, as if the air itself were bruised. I didn't feel

I possessed a body at all. I couldn't move. I couldn't speak. The air wouldn't give way to anything that could be breathed. The red and the brown were all about me. Maybe I was still asleep. I wanted very much to believe I was still asleep. Then I wondered when someone, some creature or god, might enter and make itself known. I always thought of a critical care unit as being white, sterile, and brightly lit. Where was I? I felt I was in a bad version of Dante's hell.

Maybe I was dreaming. Was there someone in my room? I tried to call out and tell him I needed a drink of water, but it was a shadow and shadows have no language. Maybe I was dead. Maybe someone had joined me in being dead. I prayed I was dead.

A young, dark haired man had entered the room or had always been there standing beside me, but I hadn't been able to see him. I saw, or thought I saw, his lips moving as if he was talking, but only many seconds later did I hear what he was saying.

I tried to see if I recognized the voice as he said to me, "It was during the Oakland Hills fire. He was working at the stables, taking care of the horses in those days."

I told him that all I needed was a drink of water. But he wouldn't look at me, and when he did look at me, he had no face. Or if he had a face, I couldn't see his face. It must have been the drugs I was on. I was accustomed to a type of life where events had explanations. I believed the more explanations, the more real the real became. The stranger continued talking to me.

"There were warnings on the radio and from the police saying that all the horses might have to be evacuated because the fire was getting dangerously close. He spent the entire night keeping watch, ready to evacuate whenever the necessity arose."

"Who?" I tried to say. "Who are you talking about?" But the ghostly figure would not answer me.

"He was standing in his white shirt, looking out over the hills, a red glow in his face, just looking. He was as much a part of the fire as he was a part of what the fire could potentially burn down."

"Who are you talking about?" I wanted to yell, my throat was so dry I could barely get the words out and not sure he even understood what I was saying.

The man was standing by my bed fiddling with the instruments on the wall high above my head. He said to me, "He was a part of neither reality, yet a part of both. Ken became the fire, standing in his white shirt, facing out into the distance. It was as if he was the distance itself."

"Who?" I wanted to scream, but I couldn't scream. And then I remembered. Ken was the man Mary had married, after I'd left her. How did this person know about him? He stood over me, taking my pulse.

"Who are you?" I asked.

"No one," he answered.

"Who in the hell are you? Answer me."

"Life begins when we give up all of the self," he answered staring at me and putting a hand gently over my eyes. "Do you remember him? It was Ken who was standing beside you, telling you that you must not look away, not hide, even though you wanted so desperately to hide. He told you to look at yourself, at others, and not be afraid. He told you to open your eyes and see."

The man turned and moved away from the bed. I must have been dreaming but it felt so real. I pressed hard on the button to call the nurse as he stood in the doorway and addressed me one last time.

"Stories are being played out over and over again, all wanting to be understood," he said, and was gone.

14

My nurse came quickly. Pushing a cart, she smiled and picked up my chart from the end of the bed. She flipped through the pages, and with a nod of satisfaction said, "Your doctor will be in a bit later, Mr. Rogers. He's very happy with your surgery. I'm just going to take a little blood. Okay?"

∞ 2 ∞

My doctors considered the surgery successful, but my condition did not improve. After a year of convalescence, severe swelling in my legs and shortness of breath forced me to go on government disability. The doctors called my condition chronic, congestive heart failure, as well as constrictive pericarditis. After surgery and months of pain, they told me they had done all they could. The pain was deeper than ever.

During my supposed convalescence, I would sit in my chair, so depressed and terrified that I would not move. I wouldn't even get up to go to the bathroom or to pick up the phone and call for help. The pain was the greatest when I stood or tried to walk. Bending over was out of the question. I did feel better when I talked with Mary, my ex-wife. She had been calling weekly since my surgery, nagging me into a better mood if I let her.

"We have an idea," she said during one of her calls, chipper as ever. Mary was always having chipper ideas. Her attempts to cheer me up escalated as chances of my recovery became more vague. "Ken might be able to help you," she said.

Ken was her new husband. At the mention of his name, I remembered the time I awoke after the surgery.

"I don't need his help," I answered.

"Now just listen. This is a serious job offer, Daniel. Ken wants to know if you would like to come to Texas and live with us? He wants to use your skills as a writer," she said. "You won't have to pay room or board." Long pause. "Well, what do you think, Dano?"

The receiver was wet with sweat from my hands. "Mary, you are out of your mind?"

"Think about it," she said, "you don't have to give me an answer now. I know Ken and you are really different kinds of people, but why not take a shot at it? You can always go back to California, right?" She waited before adding with a laugh, "It does sound weird, doesn't it."

"He'd be better served finding someone else to write for him," I said. "For God's sake Mary, why is he asking me, of all people?"

"Ask him."

"I'm really not up to doing or receiving favors from your new husband, Mary. Can't you understand that?"

"Look Danny," she said, "I know it sounds crazy, but I promised Ken I would deliver this offer to you. Take it or leave it. We have a room for you complete with television, rocking chair, and an adjustable, hospital bed."

"Mary, did your husband visit me at the hospital?"

Mary didn't answer. Then she said, "Well, Ken didn't visit you, but I was wondering when you were going to mention your visit. I'll explain the whole thing to you later, if you ever get to Texas."

"No, tell me now. I know Ken had something to do with it and if you expect me to live with the man I have a right to know. It felt very strange, surreal. There was this phantom man and I thought it all was some drug induced dream haze I was in."

"That was Paul."

"Who's Paul, may I ask?"

"A friend of Ken's. Paul said he visited you in the hospital just after your heart surgery."

"Then he wasn't a ghost," I said.

"Well, I guess he is and he isn't. Paul's had an interesting past. In 1943, the U. S. Navy conducted an experiment on a ship. Paul was one of the men aboard. You developing agoraphobia as a child is one of the reasons that Paul believes he has a connection with you."

"What are you talking about? What does being an agoraphobic have to do with ships? Okay Mary, are you playing therapist? Is this course work for Advanced Dream Interpretation 101?"

"It's just an idea, Rogers," she said and continued, "Look Daniel, if you can't leave your chair, how am I ever going to get you to Texas?"

I paused for a moment considering her offer and took the leap. What the hell I concluded, and told her, "Well, I could take a double dose of my medication and jump really fast onto a plane. Free room and board sounds enticing at the moment. But look Mary, no promises until I feel the situation out in Texas, Okay?"

"Okay. We'll be taking a trip soon so you can feel the place out all by yourself and the dog will keep you company. That will work out really well. Danny, are you still on those anti-depressants?"

"Yeah, my doctor expects I'll be on them the rest of my life. I'm an extreme case since they think my agoraphobia began when I was between two and four years old."

"So what exactly did they say about your condition?"

"Well, they acknowledged that emotionally it's almost impossible for me to go anywhere new without really freaking out."

"What does that mean?"

"If I go somewhere I haven't been before, or don't feel comfortable about, I panic. I feel I'm going to die. Really. I can't move, I can't breathe."

"Why didn't you ever tell me about this, Danny? How come I never noticed you freaking out?"

There was a long silence. "Nobody noticed, Mary, not even yours truly. I went through my life making believe nothing was wrong, until I couldn't stand it any longer and went into therapy. My therapist figured it out."

"Wow. I never would have thought you had that problem," she said and we both fell silent for a moment before she continued. "Danny, do you have any memories of being four years of age, of anything that happened back then? Ken and Paul think they know something about your past. Maybe Ken really can help you."

"Did they divine this from a rock? Tell Ken that I don't need his help, just the room and board and someone to pick me up off the floor, if I faint."

She answered with a quick, "Yeah, yeah, we'll drag your ass off the floor," and then continued more deliberately, "Now, just listen to me for a moment, okay? I know your uncle was in the Navy in 1943 and you were living in Philadelphia back then, right? The Naval experiment in 1943, was called the 'Philadelphia Experiment'. It was during the war and they were looking for a way to make a Naval vessel radar unvisible to the Japanese. Some major geniuses at the time were involved in this. Anyway, the whole idea was based on the relationship between time, space, matter and electro-magnetics. The ship actually became invisible to the eye, Danny. According to reports from men aboard, time had no meaning. They felt as though time stood still, froze, and they were stuck. Some men were actually caught between dimensions, half of their bodies melded into the ship's floor or a gun turret. All the men aboard reported a greenish fog and a buzzing sound at the moment the electro-magnetic generators were turned on and the experiment began.

"A few hours later, the ship returned and during those missing hours it appeared in Norfolk, Virginia, some four hundred miles away. Are you following this, Danny? There's more. Some of the men jumped overboard when the experiment first began and they landed, not in the sea, but in time's 'vortex' and were sent ahead in time. All the men on that ship were never the same. Many ended up in mental hospitals and Paul was one of those."

"Mary, Mary, Mary, come on," I interrupted, not being able to listen any longer. "My uncle had nothing to do with invisible ships. He was a doctor. I was four when I last saw him. I remember it, too. He was getting dressed in his uniform and I was lying on the bed pretending to be asleep. He took me on an outing, I can't remember where, and that was it. End of story."

∞ 3 ∞

The next day I went to the small local library and looked up the Philadelphia Experiment. All I found was a single reference, stating that the ship vanished because a vortex in space and time had been created. What the hell did a vortex in space and time mean? I had no idea and it intrigued me. There wasn't much to read and I quickly got bored and dropped the whole subject.

A month later I had made all my moving arrangements and managed, somehow, to get to the airport. When the plane had lifted into the air I ordered two scotches from the flight attendant and drank them with my tranquilizers and anti-depressants. Not a good idea. I took yet another dose of my tranquilizers preparing myself to see Mary again. I watched the checkerboard of land outside the window. I watched the flight attendant's legs. If I was insane, going to Texas to live with my ex-wife and her husband was surely evidence of such mental unhinging. I was trying to recall specifically what had happened to me upon awakening from surgery. I could remember the stained sheets, the walls of the room, and the ghostly presence I was trying to converse with. I knew my hallucinations had something to do with Ken, but I didn't know what. Why had I been thinking about him, of all people?

When the airplane landed in San Antonio, I walked down the orange colored tunnel into the bright cool air of the terminal. I saw Mary standing beside a white haired man, both of them waving at me. I knew I had seen him before. Maybe I had had a vision.

The next thing I remember is the light blue Lincoln Towne Car sailing through the countryside past stone houses, longhorn cattle, Spanish goats and open fields of oak and cedar. We were headed home, to a little town in the hills of central Texas called Wimberley.

We entered a subdivision of more stone homes and huge old oak trees and pulled up to a modern style white frame and stone home with a high peaked roof. Ken and Mary helped me inside to my room and unloaded my boxes of books, speaking in hushed tones and laughing together. I could hear them in the living room as I dozed off in my rocking chair, totally exhausted.

I awoke hours later. Mary had covered me with a blanket and left a sandwich on my side table. It was dark outside but a full moon illuminated my room enough for me to look around my new home. I was in a large square room. There was a long black table sitting along one wall, loaded with a hundred video and audio tapes, neatly stacked and labeled. I had my own black Sanyo television and VCR, a tape deck and radio. A white book case sat beside the large La-Z-Boy rocking chair I was sitting in. I couldn't breathe and my chest ached if I had to lie down flat, so I'd been sleeping upright in a rocking chair for the last few years. Ken and Mary found an adjustable hospital bed for me to try and that piece of furniture dominated the room. I'd love to be able to sleep in a bed again.

Along one wall of my room, was a sliding glass door, looking out over paradise. A covered wooden deck overlooked a creek draped with twiggy trees, and hills off in the distance disguising the horizon, the hills pointing to the unimaginable hugeness of the sky. The night's moon shown in the creek's shimmering, green waters, dotted with clusters of white, squawking ducks.

A glass ball on a black stand was in one corner of my room atop a dresser. It was switched on and gave out thin streams of multi-colored light. The color blue was haunting, especially following the intensity of the fiery red. I would wait for it, trying to think of what the blue orb reminded me. I saw it reflected in the sliding glass door suspended above the river like a fake aqua moon. Then with a change of perspective it became a blue planet illuminated on the glass or rather, it seemed to be coming in from the outside until it was hanging a few feet from my face. Then the colors would blend and shift and the blue planet would shatter.

Also inside my room, sitting quietly a few feet away and staring at me, was an eight month old black and white Border Collie named Polarity. We had met briefly upon my arrival and he had staked himself at my side. I didn't expect to find him still in my room. He seemed full of dogmatic opinions and began sharing them all with me now that I was awake and at his disposal. He was evidently used to snuggling close to someone, say in an extra spacious bed, and he had not, in any way, prepared himself for sleeping in a rocking chair. As soon as he had my attention, he began his assault on my lap, sure that this was the place he wanted to spend the night. The problem was how to fit dog and human in a rocking chair together. Polarity was to prove remarkable in his relentless search for the one correct position: head out of the chair, ass out of the chair, ass and head in the chair with tail wagging in my face. His tail wouldn't stop wagging. Head beside my cheek, feet in my mouth, head sunk deep into my crotch. Time to give up and sleep on the floor on top of my feet. Five minutes later, it would be time to try again.

Tired of the onslaught, I held the sliding glass door open, Polarity trotted out and the hot, humid Texas night air rushed in, paralyzing me. Only when I closed the door did he demand to be let back in, as if we had been apart for years. Then we would proceed through the spasmodic fury of the greeting process called 'where-have-you-been-all-my-life', followed by the renewed search for how human and dog could occupy the same space. Somehow, we made it through the rest of the night together.

At breakfast the next day I told Mary how exhausted I was and she understood I needed time to myself. She and Ken barely made a sound and mostly stayed in their bedroom, with Mary coming out into the kitchen to fix a meal now and then or to help Ken pack one of his suit cases for the trip they were about to take. As for Ken during those first few days, I hardly ever saw him. Mary and I hardly spoke about him either, for she was too busy showing me the house and telling me how to care for both the house and the dog while they were gone.

"Now tell me again how long you're going to be in Europe?" I queried her for the nth time.

"Six weeks," she answered staring at me. "Is your health good enough to stay here by yourself? Really, Danny? Don't bullshit me now. I know how you are." She continued to look at me as though my face would reveal more than my words.

"I think I'm okay."

Then began Mary's litany of phone numbers. Mary gave me every conceivable phone number of every conceivable service I might need while they were away on their European voyage. There were people to drive me around if I was too sick to drive, doctors close by, veterinarians even closer. There were people to help take care of the house, the dog and the lawn plus a string of long, puzzling telephone numbers where they could be reached in England, Ireland, or Sweden. She recited, copied and recopied this litany of telephone numbers and their usage any number of times, the ending line being, "Are you sure you're going to be okay all by yourself?"

I answered that I would not be by myself, since the dog seemed to be constantly with me, if not a part of me. Now and then Ken would make an appearance to double check whether I had the telephone numbers of all the doctors I might need during his absence. His long white hair and carefully trimmed white beard were striking, setting off his large, almost childlike blue eyes. Then he would remind Mary of something he wanted done or needed and it would take her the rest of the afternoon to accomplish the task.

On their last night at home, we had a large dinner and sat in the living room to watch a movie. It was called *The Philadelphia Experiment* and was about the Navy incident in 1943 that Mary had mentioned to me and that I had so unsuccessfully researched. I knew something was up and kept my mouth closed. The movie explained how the Navy attempted to make one of their Destroyer Escorts radar invisible and succeeded in making it invisible not only to radar, but to human beings as well. The remainder of the film traced the goings on of two of the survivors as they attempted to cope with the fact that at one instant they were in 1943, and seconds later were plopped down in a barren field in the year 1983. Was I supposed to intuit something from all this?

Ken seemed intent on my reactions to this movie and asked me what I thought during a break when Mary went to make popcorn.

"Well, I'm not sure what I think. This is a movie and who knows what's true," I answered him, trying to make light of the whole thing and really not wanting to get into a discussion about whether I believed any of this hollywood hype, which I didn't.

I could feel him watching me and he said, "You know, there's been quite a bit written about this incident and some of the statements by Carlos Allende have stayed with me. Allende said that the men aboard the ship referred to the state of invisibility as a 'hell incorporated' and a 'getting stuck'. And when a man is stuck, Allende advised that you go to the man and put your hands on him because, '. . . that man is the very most desperate of men in the world.'"

Just then Mary returned with bowls of popcorn and mugs of hot chocolate and we returned to the movie. When it ended, we all went to bed without another comment on the strange film. If I had known I was going to have the following dream, I would have found some reason to stay up late that night and discuss the virtues and failings of time travel, which Ken seemed to know something about, or I never would have turned on the blue glass ball. But one cannot anticipate dreams.

The Dream

The planet called Alnilam, the middle star in the belt of Orion, is where the criminals of the planet earth, frozen for eons of time, would be sent for re-education into the life of the new world. Capital punishment had been done away with and in its place was a form of suspended animation by freezing for upwards of one thousand years, depending upon the length of time the court decreed. When at last the criminals were brought back to life, it would seem to them as if only a moment in time had passed, but soon it would become apparent that they were now members of a new humanity they knew not of, a cosmos they couldn't have imagined, not unlike what faced the hero of the movie, The Philadelphia Experiment. In my dream, I was outside looking in, at a character who was me and was not me. His name too, was Daniel.

Daniel's first glimpse of that distant, magnificent blue suspended orb convinced him he must be in a motion picture theater viewing the orb on a big screen. He couldn't believe how comfortable he felt, how close the motion picture screen seemed, how much a part of the image he felt himself to be. He couldn't turn his attention away from the amazing blue orb totally surrounded by coal black space. Other than the blue orb, he felt alone.

Yet something was wrong. He heard a silence, a silence as thick as the black space itself. He needed to move, to hear his own breath, his pulse, his heart beat, any sound at all that would break the silence. It crushed in on him. He wanted to, but could not, scream out.

Just as he thought he was about to lose consciousness, the blue planet began to accelerate, without warning. Suddenly there was an explosion and he felt himself traveling through a corridor of fire. Further explosions hurled him deeper and deeper into fire and light.

He had yet to blink, as when a ball is hurled at your face, you blink. He felt the blink coming into his eyes. He felt the impulse of his head to twist away. All of his physiology told him what was happening, yet the reflex of blinking and turning away continued to well up in his senses without release. Then blue sky kissing an horizon of rolling white craters filled the screen. He blinked and turned his head.

Was that explosion of light the injection that would put him to sleep for his sentence of one thousand years, the punishment for his unspeakable crime? He remembered the last words the doctor had told him. He had been a white faced little man and his last words were a whispered, "It will be a world you won't recognize, a world you won't be able to understand." Now he understood those words. To others, his imprisonment of a thousand years, was endless. To him, the prisoner traveling near the speed of light, it had been but the blink of an eye, a blink he couldn't even remember.

He wanted to laugh. So long he had feared his punishment and now it seemed like hardly any punishment at all. He wasn't in a movie theater gazing at a giant screen; he was in a capsule with viewing windows, headed for his new home and one thousand years had passed.

There was no sensation of landing or of getting out of a vehicle, rather it was the experience of suddenly seeing images opening up on all sides of him. What he had seen as white cloud like structures, were now patterns of light in water, the water of a river, the reflection of the sun in a river. Maybe they had always been the sun in the river.

Now he could turn his head. On all sides of him were rocks and leafless trees. It had all been a dream, a thousand year old dream if the doctor had been correct. Had they thawed him out and placed him in this most idyllic setting only to punish him? Was it possible a thousand years had passed and there were still rivers and sun and sky and leafless trees? Up above was the cloud filled sky he had been looking at. He had thought for an instant it was the surface of some planet he had been flying over. How silly. All the while he could have been lying here on earth, looking up at the sun burning through the clouds. He was glad he had regained his senses.

There was an island in the river's stream of about a hundred yards in length and perhaps twenty yards wide. This island was populated with the same rocks trees and grass and a little blue shack which at first looked too small to be a shack, but rather was the size of a child's playhouse. To the rear of where he lay was a hill dotted with trees poking deep into the cloudy, low sky. On either side of him, and as far as the eye could see, were rocks and oak trees and far off bluish hills.

He wondered what he was supposed to do now and decided that the safest thing was not to move lest his new pastoral reality become altered. Was this supposed to be the place where he would be re-educated? Was he now supposed to find food and shelter, to become a poor imitation of Robinson Crusoe? Maybe he was the new Adam, without sin in the garden of Eden.

He asked himself whether he was hungry and the answer was no. He asked himself if he had any physical needs at all and the answer was still no. He felt he could lie here forever, in his present state of having no needs, and wait until someone came along to begin his re-education back into the civilized world. It sure looked like he was back on the planet earth, but after what Daniel had just been through, he wasn't sure of anything. He made up his mind to wait. He had been told he would be sent to Alnilam. Well if he was, it sure looked like planet earth in the days before the trees and vegetation died.

His attention kept being drawn to the island and to the children's playhouse, painted blue. It was either just large enough for a child to hide in or it was too small for anything other than to store tools in. Because it was the only creature-made object in view, it continued to hold his attention. Maybe Alnilam was the new Garden of Eden, populated by aliens the size of a three year old child. The idea amused Daniel. Maybe Alnilam was the land of dolls. After an hour or so he tried to determine the position of the sun in the sky, so he could tell when night would fall. But if there was a sun in the sky, it was hidden. If the sun was hidden, how could the water be shimmering with those crystal patches of light?

Daniel had no idea how much time had passed. The sky was not getting darker. He was getting bored and longed for sleep to help pass the time. If boredom was their idea of punishment, they were brilliant. He wondered if he had time before night fell to wade or swim out to that blue playhouse on the island. He liked to swim and the more he felt his boredom, the more he decided that the only way to relieve it was to go towards the only structure that was in sight. He kept telling himself to get up and move, to not be afraid.

The river was blazing with crystalline patches of light so that the island appeared to be surrounded by crystals of all shapes and sizes. Quickly, he divested himself of his uniform. He touched the water with one toe, walked gingerly in and then began to swim.

Why was he so sure he had gone forward in time? If he had been traveling at the speed of light, couldn't he have just as well gone backwards in time? And what would be the indications to tell him whether he had traveled backwards or forwards? If you don't know where you are, where is backwards and where is forwards? It wasn't more than five strokes before he found himself *walking up onto the tall grasses maybe twenty feet from the child's playhouse.*

What he had called a playhouse was a little larger than he had suspected, maybe large enough to allow one person to sit, but not to stand or lay down. As he walked towards it he saw something white in a window. He called out a tentative hello, hoping there was someone inside he could talk to. There was no answer.

When he reached the white object he saw that it was a white piece of paper. He pushed the paper aside.

"Don't do that."

"Is anyone in there?" he asked excitedly.

"No," came the answer in a distinctly female voice, sounding irritated.

"Are you also a prisoner?" he said. "I will leave you alone if you can answer that one question."

"I am being re-educated," came the answer crisply.

"Me too," Daniel laughed. "I just arrived. So, where are we?"

"You said just one question and you would leave me alone. That is what you said."

"Okay," Daniel said. "Just as long as I know someone else is alive. Where are we?" He thought for a moment. Maybe he was better off not knowing. "My clothes are on the further shore, so I guess I should return to them." He paused. "If you ever want to talk, just give me a yell. Sometimes it's nice to have someone to talk to."

There was no response.

Daniel returned to the water of a thousand dazzling crystals and the further shore of trees, rocks, and grass from whence he came. The sun, or whatever, was still giving off light. He decided to let his body dry before he put back on his white shirt and trousers. Assuming that voice was a she, and assuming the she was human, (and the fact she spoke English, probably was a good hint) soon enough she would have to come out of her playhouse. Meanwhile, he could wait. If she was human this wouldn't be such a bad place to get himself politically or morally re-educated. At least there was a presence around, which made his isolation far less bothersome. He felt a tightness in his chest. The last thing he wanted, under his current conditions, was to get sick.

He still wasn't sleepy and sleep would have been such an excellent way to pass the time. Yet he wasn't cold and he also wasn't hungry. The fact the sun wasn't setting seemed to indicate that wherever he was, it wasn't planet earth. Maybe he had been in a space ship. Maybe the light would stay this way for years and that suited him fine.

He had asked the doctor how long his re-education would take, and either the doctor wasn't suppose to tell him, or he didn't know. He started to walk, figuring it would be hard to get lost as long as he kept to the river's edge. Yet no matter how far he went, the landscape never changed. The island floating mid stream had long since been left far behind, but that was the only difference he was aware of. If it hadn't been for the island and that shack, he could have sworn he hadn't moved at all. If there was food about, he didn't recognize it as food. Maybe there was a root one could eat, but which root?

Finding nothing of use to him, he quickly made his way back to where he had begun, the idea suddenly coming to him that she might have left the shack while he was gone. This idea alarmed him, made him break into an all out run. He only had his sandals on, otherwise he was naked. He started to run. Even when he was out of air and his chest was burning as if it was on fire, he ran.

And just as he was about to give up and rest he spotted the island in the distance. The sight gave him a new burst of energy, and he sprinted the rest of the way, calling to her. There was no answer.

Why had he not stood guard over her he thought, calling out again and again. Mindlessly, he plunged into the water and swam out to the island, scrambling up onto the shore, determined to make sure some life form was still there. He banged on the shack, demanding to know if she was inside.

"Go away," the voice finally said. "You promised."

He breathed a deep sigh of relief; she was still there. "I would do better if you would talk to me. I'm from the third planet from the sun. Where are you from?"

Daniel could hear her laughing.

"Is it nice in there?" he asked. "Are you also from the third planet from the sun?"

"Which sun?" the distinctly female voice asked.

Daniel thought for a moment. How was he suppose to know which sun? "Does the Milky Way mean anything to you?" he asked. Again he heard her giggle.

"That was a long time ago," she said still giggling. "I mean, the Milky Way was a long time ago."

"How can the Milky Way be a long time ago?" Daniel asked with a laugh.

"I studied about the Milky Way in school," said she.

"You don't suppose I can see your face?" he asked.

"The Milky Way was a long time ago," she said. "Which means you never went to school, or you would have known."

"Known what?"

"That something happened to it."

"Why do you say that? I mean that something happened to it. Very funny," Daniel quipped. "If we are so far away that something could have gone wrong with the Milky Way, then where in the hell are we?"

"On the only thing that's left, stupid."

"Come on, be serious. Alnilam is in the Milky Way."

"Find something else," said the irritated voice.

"Look, how in the hell do you know the Milky Way has disappeared?"

"Inner realization," she said. "You're one of those 'thousand year' guys, right? You were to be frozen for a thousand years, but you never bothered to ask how long a year would be in a thousand years. Did you ask any of the really pertinent questions?"

"What the hell does that mean?"

"A thousand years is a geographical reference. It means one thing one place and another thing another place. I bet you are one of the ones who never stopped to think about that. Anyway where we are is plenty far enough away for the Milky Way to have gone poof. Maybe it has gone poof more than once."

"I don't believe you. What kind of poof?"

"A poof kind of poof."

"I beg to differ. The Milky Way was plenty big. It must have done more than go poof."

"Then why did they all leave?" she asked calmly.

"They? Who's they?"

"All of them. I can't tell you everyone who 'they' is. You shouldn't expect that of me."

"I don't believe you."

"Look, I could really care less. They didn't tell me my re-education was going to be filled with humanistic blubbering about such nonsense."

"So where did they go?" Daniel asked.

"Took them a long time to find a place for us to be re-educated. Took them a hundred light years, but they finally found this wretched place, away from everyone else. It got crowded and so the Milky Way went poof."

"You don't know what you're talking about. I might believe all your stuff if I could see what you look like." He waited, and then with a voice filled with a new concern, said, "I think this is all a big put on."

She was laughing. "You have plenty of time to think that if you want to think that."

"I damn well want to think that."

"In a few thousand years you're going to get bored with thinking that."

"And I suppose you have been here more than a few thousand years."

"I told you, a year depends on where you are. I have heard in some places a year is a million times longer than I think it is here."

"And how long do you think it is?"

"Well," she began, "it used to be thirteen twenty-eights using the earth sun as a reference point, of course."

"How in the hell do you speak English so well."

"Energy," she announced. "Language is nothing but energy, or did your school not even teach you that."

"My energy?" Daniel asked. "You are saying you are picking up my energy and my energy is English?"

"Damn right it is. And it's the stupidest kind of energy. Totally linear is what it is. Damn linear. Boring. No *wonder you are afraid of being bored." She waited. "I heard rumors about you guys from the Milky Way. A heathen lot."*

"And you? You're not a heathen lot? You're here to be re-educated, just like I am, aren't you?"

"Of course. Why else would I be talking to a creature from the Milky Way. Dear man, you have a long way to go. My God, you don't even know about your homeland going poof. The residents had a lot of prior notice that the 'poof' was going to happen. So what happened? They go out and infect the rest of the universe with their baser, linear, dreamless kinds of energy."

"See, I knew you weren't enlightened. An enlightened person wouldn't say that."

"Very low on the soul growth ladder," she said giggling. "I know. My great, great, great grandfather was from that piddling linear way of thinking. Which is probably why I ended up here. Don't worry. It's only boring and lonely for the first million years. After that, the you disappears and what's left gets used to it."

In a fit of rage, Daniel tore away the white paper, determined to see who or what was inside the shack. Behind the white paper was a computer screen that covered the window and on the screen were letters that read "File: PASTORAL." And down in the right hand corner of the screen were the words "Press ESC to escape. Press ENTER to continue."

"It's your choice," said a giggly voice from the corner of the shack. "Either you can press ESC, that means maybe death, or ENTER. Once I pressed ENTER and I was asked if I was sure I wanted to continue. I wasn't sure I wanted to continue but I pressed ENTER anyway."

"What happened?" Daniel asked, beginning to feel himself awaken from what he now was sure was a dream. "This is madness..."

"The screen gave me a choice. I could select CRYSTALS or YUCATAN or HELP."

"And you selected?"

"I selected HELP," the voice said. "I didn't know what the rest of the words meant. So I decided to play it safe. And I got you. And then, to make matters worse, the screen flashes PLEASE WAIT at me. Do you know how long I have been waiting? Lousy program. While I'm waiting, the software lectures me. It says things like, 'All acts of giving will be, in the future, a crime. All acts of stealing will be seen as devotion to our God. Our fathers and mothers will become the only enemy we can depend upon. Greed will be seen as the ultimate success and it will be taught in every school as the secret to salvation of the soul and the body. Killing and sex will become all that our art forms will be about. Brutality will be what the definition of the beautiful and the sexual are since we won't be able to feel anything else. Then the messiah will come upon the scene and brilliantly save us from ourselves. He will show us that we are the gods and we had better act like it." She took a deep breath.

A long deliberate pause. "And humanity begins all over again."

"What begins all over again?"

"The Milky Way, I mean all human life. Hasn't it occurred to you as yet?"

"Hasn't what occurred to me?"

"The danger we are in, the danger of beginning the whole damn thing all over again?"

Daniel asked, "What danger are we in? What danger of beginning what all over again?"

"If we are the only ones on this planet, the danger is transcendent," said she. "If we should see each other and, like Adam and Eve fall in love, civilization, damn it, begins all over again. We are the only two on the planet and we could give birth to a third." She waited. "It isn't worth the pain. Therefore, I am going to have to kill you. I mean, don't take it personally, but the universe can't afford for it to begin all over again."

"So we are on earth," I said. "You lied to me about the Milky Way."

"We are on the verge of creating not only a new human race, but crystals which will store our dreams, and all that never was. Adam," she called, "press ESC. It will be far easier that way. Just press ESC. And when they ask if you are sure that you want to exit the program, don't think. Tap Y for yes."

∞ 4 ∞

Mary's anxious voice was coming from the doorway of my bedroom. Ken was standing behind her saying that Mary's computer had just crashed. He didn't seem at all bothered by the electronic catastrophe.

"I think my screams of distress woke him up," Mary said to Ken, coming in and sitting down on my bed. I didn't know how long I had been asleep, but it seemed like forever.

"I just had the oddest dream..." I wasn't awake enough to finish the sentence. I hadn't washed my hair. I must look like hell. "I was dreaming about spaceships and computers, of all things."

"Makes sense to me," Mary began, "You must have heard my ravings from the next room. I was sending out distress calls to all my computer friends. Maybe that's why you were dreaming about computers."

"So that's who the girl was in the shack on the island."

"What island?" Mary asked. "What girl?"

"It was you. It was exactly like that shack we had once lived in, in Point Reyes."

"It must have been small," Mary said with a laugh, backing up into Ken's arms, who was stationed behind her. "The only trouble is, we didn't have a computer in those days." She bumped Ken with her rear end and said, "Ken wants to know if you want to go out for breakfast with us. We have just enough time before we leave."

"You're not here as a patient," Ken began. "We brought you here to write, so I think it's about time you hear what it is we want you to write about."

"He means the Yucatan story," Mary said, looking at her wrist watch. "Ken, I don't know if we have time for the entire story."

"Then what's he going to do for six weeks?" he asked.

"He's going to get better," Mary said. It was more of a demand than a statement.

"The Yucatan," I blubbered. "That was one of the selections on the computer, the computer in my dream."

"What computer?" Mary asked. Then she remembered something crucial she had forgotten to pack, and wondered out loud how cold it was going to be in London as she hurried out of the room. I decided that whatever the coincidence was concerning the Yucatan, I didn't have the wits to explore it at any length.

"What do you think that dream meant?" Ken was asking, his lips twitching up into a smile. "If it was totally outrageous, then you know there's a truth there for you."

"Well, this was totally outrageous," I said. What was he trying to infer? Was he pulling my leg?

Mary was calling Ken, asking him to call for the weather in London. Ken stuck out his open palm, as though checking for rain, and called back, "Fair and cool. Zero percent chance of precipitation."

"You don't suppose God is an Apple computer do you?" I asked facetiously.

"Ah, compatibility difficulties and all. That's an interesting simile," he laughed. "Well, I'll say good-bye to you now. I should give Mary a hand."

"You really mean you want me to write a book?" I paused. "Do I have to become a believer?"

"It would have been easy to get a believer to write a book, but not the book I have in mind."

"Which is?"

"Anyone can write about boats vanishing, like in that movie we saw."

"Are we going out for breakfast or not?" Mary called. "Ken, do you know where my jacket is? The leather one?"

"The dog took it," I answered.

"Mr. P., my love, tell me it isn't so," Mary pleaded.

"Daniel," Ken said, "I want you to write a book about reality going poof. You don't believe that can happen, do you?"

Mary reappeared and interrupted our conversation saying, "Let's go to breakfast, guys. I'm starved."

Over breakfast at the Cypress Creek Cafe, I told Ken about the books I had written, all of which had the same theme. My first was actually a poetic travel diary about a wandering Buddhist monk; the second was a novel about Jesus, also a traveler and teacher, that I was working on when I was married to Mary. The traveler/scholar theme had obsessed me at that time. Now from what Ken was saying, he seemed to be asking me if I'd like to write a third book on the same theme.

Ken paid the bill and we were back at the house long before the car arrived to take them to the airport. "Why do you want me, of all people, to write this book?" I yelled as Ken got into the back seat of the station wagon.

He leaned his head out of the window, reading my mind, "You are also a traveler, Daniel. You just don't know it."

∞ 5 ∞

I thought about going to get something to drink, about taking a shower, about trying to watch some of the video tapes of Ken's work. Instead, I went into my bedroom, sat in my rocker and stared at the sunlit crystals flashing in the river, and fell asleep.

Yet Another Dream

In my mind, the glass ball had turned a deep blue and expanded in size. It rose up, pulsating, as if it was alive and breathing. The blue ball formed lips and eyes. I wondered where all the light in the room had gone. Then I was once again in the little shack on the island in the middle of the river. This time it was a male voice I heard. On the computer screen was a file named YUCATAN. I pressed ENTER.

"Where am I?" I shouted at the computer.

"Her name was Cradle Flower. She was a medicine woman," said the male voice of the monitor.

"I asked you, where am I? I have to know."

"You will find out in good time," said the voice I now recognized as Ken's. "There's a story I have to tell you."

"I'm not going to press ESC, if that's what you want. Where is she?"

"I'm not talking about her. I'm talking about a medicine woman. Listen to me. The particular tribe she was a member of would not enter the cemetery."

On the screen appeared a crowded cemetery, filled with ghosts and spirits and voices of the dead and the voice droned on:

"Because they cannot enter the graveyard, the tribe has others that bury their dead. One day, a group went in to clean up the cemetery. The grounds had not been weeded for a long time and some of the crosses on the graves had fallen over. They gathered up all the crosses and stacked them next to the little part of the church that was left there, with the bell tower, but nobody had marked where the crosses had originally been and it was sort of a joke because they didn't know how to put the crosses back in place after they'd weeded and cleaned up. Next to the church wall all you could see were stacks and stacks of little crosses.

"This tribe felt that once the spirit left, the body was unimportant. Time no longer mattered. Cradle Flower could move in and out of her body. She could move into many dimensions. She told me one day I would know the secrets of time. 'The crystals will teach you the breath, the secrets of heaven and hell.' Maybe she was aboard that vanishing boat that sailed on the horizon far away.

"I was told that I was to find her ashes and dig them up. When I found the urn, it was mostly disintegrated. I took the urn and the pieces and some of the dirt and put it in a box with the little wooden head stone I had and I figured that I would hold it, keep it. At the cemetery that day, I had it with me and decided to take a handful of the ashes and throw them over the cemetery so that any earthbound spirits could be released. I knelt as near to her grave as I could, on the surrounding wall. They don't

allow visitors to walk in the cemetery, either. I had put a crystal there, where I knelt. No, it was not a crystal. It was a star I'd picked out of the night's sky. God had cried only once and the crystals were his tears. All of a sudden I noticed a storm getting closer and closer. It was heading down the valley from Blue Lake, this black, white, gray cloud, this huge thunderhead just coming directly toward me. The wind was starting to kick up all around. As I held a handful of her ashes, her dirt, her being, I could feel how her family had loved her. As I threw the ashes over the cemetery I told her I love her too."

The shack was now overflowing with blue light glowing out from the screen. I could feel the light's heat. I could only hear Ken's voice. Then I saw him on the monitor. This time he appeared far away, his white hair blowing in the ocean's wind as he stood on the deck of a ship, beckoning to me. His voice sounded only inches from my face, so that all he had to do was to whisper in order to be heard. Then his image faded and on the computer screen appeared the prompt, "Press ESC to escape. Press ENTER, to continue." I pressed ENTER and an image of Ken appeared. He was standing along the cemetery wall and his voice said:

"The whole cemetery came alive and all the energy and all the beings and all the spirits that had been held because of anger or hatred or confusion just shot out and upward and the clouds rolled in fast like there was a vacuum. As the spirits shot up into the clouds, lightening and thunder crashed overhead.

"By the time we got to our car, rain and thunder were coming hard, washing everything away, clearing everything, cleansing everything."

The image of Ken closed his eyes, dropped his arms to his sides, and then knelt to kiss the ground. Then the monitor was showing what appeared to be a TV commercial. I could see Ken in the midst of a Lincoln-Mercury dealership and he said:

"In the years that followed, I discovered that I was good at social life and business. So much of it is an illusion and it's easy to be good at an illusion. But at night, when you dream, it's no longer so easy. When you dream you travel into different dimensions of time, different dimensions of reality. In these, the higher dimensions, there is no such thing as control for there is nothing to control. In those days people believed in me and my projects and would advance me any sum of money. It was like I couldn't do anything wrong. I was very successful; I didn't believe there was anything money couldn't buy. I defined my success purely by how much money I made and how many toys I had. So I can tell you what it's like to have succeeded that way in this life. I didn't know what real value was. I thought it was all those plaques on my walls."

On the computer screen a fancy high powered sports car was racing along a country road. The voice over was saying words I didn't understand. As I was about to press ESC, Ken's voice said:

"I was the National Sales Manager for a printing company and I had salesmen all over the United States. The job was very easy for me. If you really believe in what you're doing and you know exactly what you want, you can feel the energy."

I banged on the ESC button three times, nothing happened. On the screen, a man dressed in a dark business suit was firing a machine gun and his sweaty face glinted in the blue light as his foe perished in front of him. Then he looked straight at me and in Ken's voice said:

"In the end like in the beginning, I was coming back to the eye, the screen, the visual image. The image of the eye was to dominate each and everything I did in my life, whether it be my holograms or my dreams. I couldn't get away from that image. It repeated itself as the vision of the large eye suspended in my hotel room in the Yucatan and the crystal I found as the eye for the gate keeper crystal. Wherever I turned it was as if the television eyes, the gate keeper eyes, Christ's blinded eyes all followed me and became my theme.

"When I was just starting out and a little guy, twenty years old, I was on a task force for General Cable. I would go into plants and totally reorganize them. I was young, but I was really good at this job. I knew how to work with people, make decisions and get things done.

"I got into product development and started my own national trading company where I went overseas and bought a product, different types of eyes called screens, and then I would do a marketing plan and sell these eyes, these screens all over the country. I wanted the eyes, the

screens to be everywhere to see into everything so that we could all learn to be one."

I covered my ears and closed my eyes, but the voice droned on relentlessly. I turned to run out of the little shack and I found myself back in my bedroom, sitting in my rocking chair. There was a huge eye ball in the corner of my room with a little tornado of wind jumping up and down and circling all around it. I covered my eyes again, pleading. "Oh, God, Oh, God. Please don't let me go mad," but Ken's voice continued:

"I had a Mercedes, a plane and a beautiful house with a swimming pool and tennis courts. Then it happened. One morning, I'm taking a shower and looking out the window and I saw it. It was a huge, bluish-white eye, the retina appearing like a dark brown translucent pool. In the center of the dark pool a pin prick of brilliant light flashed and disappeared like a distant, timeless crystal in a night's sky. Now it was this star of light, this pin prick of fiery white that seemed to be talking to me from a great distance, from thousands of miles away. The eye told me that I had lost my way.

"Transformation either happens so slowly you don't know it is happening or it explodes like a black hole, so fast you don't know what has happened to you. For me it was the latter.

"Clear Lake is nestled about one hundred miles north of San Francisco. At that time, it was an old resort community that was pretty well run down. I thought I would go there, find an older resort, fix it up and turn it into a beautiful place. And so I went up and bought a

mobile home park. In one day they said 'Yes, it's yours.' I left my job, sold my house, and moved my family.

"The park was on a beautiful creek that ran across the front of the property and cut through a thousand acre field. I didn't realize at first that for eons of time this area had been the cultural hub of a large Native American tribe. I only knew that I was supposed to be there even though my purpose was unclear to me.

"I went to work and completely remodeled the resort and still something was missing. I wasn't happy. I thought working only during the vacation season and playing with my boats would be great. In an effort to feel good, I started filling my life with more stuff. I bought more resorts and then this big, old, run down motel on the lake with twenty five rooms, a swimming pool and a bar. It was a motorcycle hang-out, but I got it for a good price.

"One month later, there were flower beds in front of my motel. Soon I had one of the most popular night clubs in Northern California and that was another short lived high. And I'll tell you, the loneliest times I ever spent were at that place at night."

"Stop it, stop it. Leave me alone," I yelled at the wind demon. All the wind can do is dwell in leafy trees, in curtains, in a woman's hair. What does the wind know of making money? I jumped out of my chair and ran from the room and the little tornado followed me into the hallway. As I got to the kitchen an even colder wind was streaming through the window above the sink and formed into yet another, bigger tornado that reached to the ceiling. I stood pressed against the sink not daring to move as the two whirlwinds had a stand off in the middle of the kitchen, the bigger one in a woman's voice, lecturing the smaller:

"You tried to buy yourself peace. You bought a three story house on the lake with a sailboat out back. You bought resorts and marinas with boats and jet skis, everything that you liked to play with. You even had mechanics to fix all your toys.

"All of that was not enough. Then suddenly everything you had was crumbling. The floods came, just as they had come in the old testament. It was the first flood in one hundred years and two of your properties went under water and one stayed under water for six weeks.

"Every day you sat there and watched until the waters started to recede, and you could get to one of your stores. And you said, 'You're not going to beat me.' You got sand bags and bagged the door, even though the store was under water, as though that was going to help. You got pumps and thought, 'I'm going to pump you out.' But you pumped and pumped and pumped and finally you submitted and let it all go.

"Two years later you had another flood. This time it took three of your resorts under water and one of the bars you had, a little mom and pop bar, and you said, 'I'm not going to close.' The bar had a foot or so of water in it, so you got sand bags and built them up right around the bar. You put the bar stools up on the sand bags and you gave the bartender hip boots and you didn't close. But your real problems had only just started. You had spent a lot of money remodeling the catalogue store to meet the new prototype that the parent company required. You had a crew there and had torn the ceiling out and put in new floors and new walls and then you get this telegram. It says, 'Dear Sir, All Montgomery Ward catalogue stores in the United States are being closed.'

"Your body felt like it was being torn into pieces and you couldn't find the pieces, couldn't get yourself back into a whole. You became a non-person, a non-husband, a non-father."

The little tornado then began to speak. He was barely jumping and twirling now and the tone of his voice, Ken's voice, was low and sad:

"Well, other people might say I lost only 'things' and 'money', but they didn't understand. It was who I was, what I kept telling myself I was, and the rest of the world kept telling me I was. Then, when I'd felt everything there was to feel, when desperation had swallowed me, there was no feeling at all, just a nothingness. I was a hollow person walking around feeling nothing and eventually thinking of nothing except how I could get even. This must have been someone else's fault.

"All during that time I kept remembering that day you took me up to your pueblo. I was just fourteen at the time, remember? We went out into a large desolate field and sat beneath a tree. You stared at me without saying a word. 'You're a spirit traveler,' you finally said. 'The crystals will teach you about energy, about time and travel.'" Oh, Cradle Flower, what had I done with my life?"

Both tornadoes then seemed to melt towards the floor and become part of the turbulent ocean's surface on which a ghost of a ship was stranded midst the pounding waves. I was no longer in the kitchen, but on the deck of that ship. Everywhere was this blueish light, and a force that wouldn't allow me to move, that sucked me into it and turned all reality into ghosts, partial shadows of what was true. Through the green mist, Ken's voice intoned the following:

"*I remember the story of Alexander the Great walking past a drunk lying in the middle of the road. I remember the day he turned to one of his advisors and said, 'That man has far more than I do.' At that time Alexander ruled the world but he understood what a burden that power was. He had sacrificed his freedom to feed his creation.*

"*I finally made a decent decision for myself and I went to a hospice and said I wanted to help. I would sweep the floors, anything. I just wanted to do something to help. I would look at those people, far worse off than I was, and I would envy them. They didn't play games, or try to be what they were not. They were forced, like I was being forced, into asking the cosmic questions: 'What's this all about? Who am I? Am I anyone at all or am I an actor playing many different roles?'*

"*It was the dying who taught me how to let go, how to confront my fears. If you know your greatest fear, go out and volunteer to work with people who also have that fear. Ask 'Who am I?' as you remove the dirty sheets from the bed, apply soothing ointments and hold their hands. There are hundreds of organizations, just find them and offer your services, clean windows, do anything, but by helping them, you are helping yourself. And ask, 'Who am I?' The people in the hospice where I worked, they were my teachers. I wasn't helping them, they were helping me. They taught me that only when you have lost everything can you possibly know who you are, because you are what is left. After everything is said and done, you are what is left.*

51

"There was this young man in the hospice, dying of AIDS. I never once heard him complain or even sound as if he were in pain though we all knew he was in bad shape. Now and again an ambulance would come for him because we were sure he was going to die. He would go away to the hospital and we would clean out his room. Then a week later, back he came to the hospice. Do you know something? I would see him sitting up in bed, doing some form of Buddhist (or at least that's what I thought it was) meditation, and as soon as anyone came into his room he would stop and appear to be just dosing, sitting up in bed as straight backed as he could. 'Very few of us ever find out anything by choice,' was the gloomiest thing I ever heard him say. The last day of his life I remember asking him how he endured the pain and he whispered, 'Learn something every day.'

"We are forced into finding answers for ourselves only when our backs are up against the wall. Now, you can't work with those who are dying of AIDS or cancer without thinking, this pain can't be the only reality there is. And then you sit and stare at the trees and the mountains and the sun reflected in the water and for one second you realize how interconnected everything is. And you ask, 'Who am I now?' Everything is exactly in the perfect place. Everything is whole and interconnected.

"I remember holding up a rock and thinking for a split second, this rock is all I need. 'Learn something every day.' The little rock turned out to be a crystal covered in dry mud. Everything is alive, even the silences. That is what the crystal was telling me. Diverse cultures from all over the world come up with the same myths, the same gods, the same magic. It's like we are all mirrors of each

other. We are stories about people telling stories about more people telling stories. Mirrors reflected in mirrors. If we are nothing but the roles we play, nothing but masks, is there anything at the core which is not a mask. 'Who am I?' a Zen monk might ask you. They say God is an onion. What is at the center of an onion? Don't think. Speak. Speak now.

"One day I stopped at a crystal store in Clear Lake. It was a little place run by an older fellow who had owned the store for twenty years. When I looked around in his display cases, I saw this wonderful onyx piece shaped like a teardrop. It looked like a pendulum and was about six or seven inches long and quite wide at the top. I asked him what it was for and he said that a man over on the other side of the lake had asked it to be carved for him a number of years ago. He was going to use it as a pendulum, but he passed away and so never picked it up. I asked the owner how much he wanted for it. He told me twenty dollars and I bought it.

"The following summer, I took that onyx pendulum with me to Mexico. That first evening I found myself in a Holiday Inn, in Merida, with my friend Paul. It was about five in the afternoon, the sun was about to set and I was out swimming in the pool. It was raining lightly and I was swimming alone thinking about this adventure I was on. Then I looked up and there were two rainbows, one above the other. Maybe I was running away. Maybe I had come to heal. Why was I here? I was in the swimming pool and I had never seen rainbows like that and to me, it was my first visual sign that I was in the right place, but for what?

"I wanted to remain in the swimming pool, waiting for the end of the rainbow. Where were my children and my *wife? Why couldn't they be here with me? What had I done to fail so badly. But Paul was talking, telling me about the first pyramid he wanted to visit. He explained that the first pyramid was the base chakra - Uxmal. I hadn't been to any pyramids since my trip to Egypt, ten years before.*

"But here I was, on a trip to Central America, to place eight crystals, representing the chakra points, in eight different pyramids. We had to visit each pyramid in a specific order and the pyramids were arranged roughly in the configuration of a fibronachi spiral. This was all Paul's plan. I came along for the adventure.

"Paul told me I wasn't acting like my old self. I told him I felt like an onion. He laughed. I was in the Yucatan feeling like an onion. I was about to be damned or saved, I didn't know which, and for the first time in my life I no longer cared.

"The next day we started for the pyramids. Uxmal was an old place. Paul looked around, trying to find the right spot to bury the crystal. I suggested we have a Koolaid instead. He laughed and we explored for a couple hours until we were sure that the general area was at the base of one of the pyramids. It was grassy there. I showed him the tear drop onyx I had with me and we suspended it with a strong clothes line rope so we could use it as a pendulum. I walked around with the pendulum and, all of a sudden, the stone came loose from the ropes and fell, sticking nose first into the ground. "Shit" was my first response as the sling broke. Then I decided that maybe the crystal wanted to be there and it was perfect.

"We then found spots and buried crystals at the second and third pyramids, Labna and Coba. After we

buried those first three crystals, I started to have this strange experience. I was not only hearing the words Paul spoke to me, I was intensely feeling what every word meant or could mean. A million possibilities flooded my consciousness. It is said that in our dreams we are everything, every person we are dreaming about, and that was the way I felt. I was partaking, not just listening, but partaking with all my senses, of what was being said.

"About three o'clock that afternoon we arrived at Chichén Itzá and started to climb the large pyramid. The sides were very steep and there were chains to help you keep your balance as you climb. When we got to the top, we noticed a storm was coming. Most of the people had cleared out. At the top there were three openings. We looked over to the front of the face of the sacred well and there was no one in there. Rain was coming down in waves with thunder and lightening.

"Each time we had put crystals in the first three pyramids it had started to rain, the rain becoming like the surface of an ocean on which we were stranded. All of a sudden this little dog came up the steps and walked in. It was a small dog about the size of a beagle. This little dog had just climbed the pyramid in this torrential downpour. I have no idea how he did it. It was so high and steep that the dog must have been hit right in the face with water. When he reached the top he shook himself off, looked at me, looked at Paul and went over and sat in the corner. He stared at me, I stared at him, we stared at each other. He scratched himself and went to sleep.

"When the storm passed we left, the dog sleeping soundly as though he no longer had to stand guard. We went next to Tulum, on the coast. As I walked, I became *aware of an energy and an awareness of things; where things were, where things would go. I started to feel sensations that I had not been consciously aware of before. As we started walking around Tulum, we got into one of the pyramids and there was another dog sitting in a corner, the same type of mongrel as before. He sat there like he knew what he was doing, like he was guarding or watching. He stared at us the entire time we were there. I told the dog to be a good dog and go to sleep. The dog didn't listen. He growled. (The dog was cold. The dog didn't say good-bye.)*

"As we climbed to the top of the pyramid, we felt we knew exactly where to go. We looked down and there was this enormous barracuda beneath us, watching and swimming back and forth, like he and the dog were guarding the pyramid from the sea. So we hid the crystal where we knew it would be safe.

"The next pyramid was partially buried. I went up to the top where there was a wall and I sat and looked down over the whole complex. The wind was blowing hard. I stretched my arms back behind me like a bird with its wings back in the wind. Then I saw a shadow and looked up and there was a large eagle about thirty feet above, doing the same thing. It just hovered above me, its wings blown back by the wind. I then had a vision. There was a triangular cave opening at the base of a tree.

"I called to Paul, 'Come over here, I know it's here.' We went to the side of the pyramid that was all covered with grass. I told him, 'We're here.' Small steps lead up the side, and at the top there was a plateau. I pointed straight ahead and told Paul, 'It's over in the corner.' As we walked over to the corner of the plateau there was a

cave in the ground. It had a triangle opening and a tree grew directly next to it. I put the crystal there and my body started to change. I felt opened up in new ways. I was keenly aware of time and space and felt both frightened and amazed. I remembered what all of us have the opportunity, on this earth, to remember. We have been here before and we have forgotten who we are and I knew there was something I was suppose to do, to be.

"Palenque was where we were to go next. The pyramid needed its eyes, needed our crystals for eyes. When got there a man was just beginning the mountain climb and we decided to go with him. It was hot, amazingly hot. We climbed two miles or so until we reached the top of the mountain and looked out over a beautiful valley where corn was planted.

"When we got to the main area of the pyramids, we separated to look around. I came upon a lemon tree and picked a fruit. As I took a knife and cut the lemon I got the worst burning sensation in my eyes. It had nothing to do with the lemon, but the lemon had triggered something. I remembered a place, I remembered a time when I'd been here, at Palenque, before.

"I sat beneath the lemon tree as old images and feelings flooded my mind and heart. Finally my eyes stopped stinging and I went up into the tower. I laid a crystal there, inside the very top. I was paying homage to the past. Again I sat by a tree and started to meditate. There was no other reality. Then it appeared. The eye was before me suspended in the air. The retina was a dark brown translucent pool. In the center of the retina, a pin prick of brilliant light flashed and disappeared like a distant, timeless star in a clear night's sky. I knew that the

light in the eye was my inner self begging me to recognize who I was and what I was to become if only I would wake up and remember.

"The next day we started for Guatemala. It took us a day and a half, and when we got to the border they wouldn't let us take our car over into Guatemala. We left our car in an hotel parking area. That night, about nine o'clock, we crossed the border.

"All around were military personnel with guns and I was nervous. We boarded a bus and after a few miles the bus was pulled over and searched. They searched all the passengers and then let us continue. Every five or ten miles on the road there were guard posts, and when we got close to one the bus driver would signal us and everybody standing in the aisle would squat down. As soon as we passed the station, they'd all stand back up. Someone finally told me that our bus was seriously overloaded with people and it was against the law to stand in the aisles. I gripped my seat for the rest of the journey, nervously jigging my leg as we drove past guard post after guard post.

"That night we stayed at an Inn and called the airport to make plane reservations into Tical. There were three, six to twelve passenger planes that left every day, but all the seats for the next day were full, and they were also fully booked for the next few days. Early the next morning we decided to go out to the airport, but the planes were still full. A group was coming in so we went to the back and sat down and decided to make two seats available for ourselves. We started concentrating. I'd never focused so intently. I needed to get home. This journey was almost done. We'd been trying to get to Tical for several days and

it had become harder and harder, like we were moving against some force. A group pulled up and we watched. All of a sudden they came and told us that two people had changed plans that morning and wouldn't be needing their reservations. Two seats were open, and we were heading out to Tical.

"We arrived about six o'clock. As we walked over to the third pyramid, a couple was there and they were playing, laughing and teasing each other. That was the energy we wanted, the energy of play. At the base of the pyramid, the plants were thick and jungle-like. Paul was ahead of me about twenty feet and, all of a sudden, the wind came around, and it was very strong. It had to be sixty, eighty miles an hour. I was holding onto two tree limbs to keep my balance, and the wind was spinning around me faster and faster. I was in an energy vortex. I could feel every particle of my body changing. I could feel energy coming from the base of my spine right up to the top of my head and I was... I was so... then I screamed as loud as I could, 'Who am I?'

"I felt energy flowing though my hands and out my fingers. My hands were hot. I was a part of the land, the air, the elements, everything. I had never felt so connected to earth. I knew who I was. 'Give it all away,' I kept telling myself. Let go, let go of what you think being human means, what you think being sane means, what you think being good means, what you think being alone forever means. Let go. I saw a greenish light, I heard the noise of the sea. When you die, your body turns into ashes, and grass grows out of those ashes, which are deep in the earth, and a cow comes along and eats the grass, and when the maiden comes to milk the cow, in order to

have milk for her child, the ashes are in the milk the child sucks. Or, the ashes fly into the wind and land on the feathers of a bird, or go deep in the ocean or even remain in the clouds and are a part of the sunset, which a poet sees, and writes about. You are alive, because you are a part of that baby's milk and poet's poem. Nothing dies in this world. Even if the planet was blown to smithereens, there will be one infinitesimal particle left behind, even if it is only a molecule, and in that molecule is all that this planet ever was or ever could be."

Now Ken sat cross legged before me on the deck of the ship, in the greenish mist. He was clicking his teeth together and saying:

"We do this in time with the beating of our hearts, which makes the heart beat slow down. The drums of the body are everywhere. The sound of teeth clicking runs down the entire course of your spine affecting all of the body with its rhythm. Who are you, Daniel? What if the flow of blood is a river, the breath is the wind? What if that bag of bones and blood we call ourselves is not solid at all but the essence of the earth, the sun, and the stars themselves. The body and the mind are nothing but frequency, the music of the sphere, as Plato said. Beating the drum of the skull is only an attempt to get in tune with the music of the sphere and deny the illusion that we are all individual selves. Instead, we are a fantastic, massive symphony, playing a tune we call a life, as simple and as misunderstood as God. Reality is but a fiction with a long pedigree and language is our god, defining our reality with her limits.

"Do you remember the story of the monk, the monk who had fallen off the edge of a hundred foot cliff. He was hanging onto a shrub which was about to give way when he saw just above him a beautiful strawberry. He knew if he reached for the strawberry he would fall to his death. I am that monk and I have decided to take the strawberry. There is only the now and the breath, here, now, always. Are you ready?"

I heard the front door unlock and I rushed groggily from my chair into the hallway. I must have dozed off after Ken and Mary left for the airport. What had Mary forgotten this time? Both of them were standing in the doorway smiling at me, their luggage piled at their feet. Why were they back? Had their plane been canceled?

Ken greeted me with a cheerful, "Hello, Daniel." Mary was blowing hair out of her face and inquiring about my health and how I liked Texas and complaining that six weeks had seemed like forever.

∞ 6 ∞

Ken brought in the suit cases and Mary said she was exhausted and cranky and needed a nap. Ken was laughing at the exuberant greeting of Polarity and spent the next twenty minutes with a joyful canine glued to his body as he tried to check the telephone's answering machine for messages. Mary plopped down at her desk and divided the huge stack of mail into smaller stacks of mail. I stood in the midst of the kitchen stroking my beard and trying to make sense out of what had happened to me.

"Gosh, it's good to be home," Ken said. "Six weeks is too long."

I still thought he had misspoken, that he had meant six hours, certainly not six weeks. But hadn't Mary said the same thing at the door when she came in?

"It couldn't have been six weeks," I said with a laugh.

"Sure didn't seem like six weeks to me," Mary said. "Seemed like six years. Well, so how did you do here all by yourself?"

"Well, fine," I said, "Except that it's impossible six weeks went by." I could hear how dogmatic I was being and thought I had every right to be dogmatic. My first thought was to blame my confusion on the medication I was supposed to be taking. Maybe the medication had caused a memory lapse.

"Danny, is something wrong?" Mary asked.

"Nothing really," I said. "I was just having a lot of long, bizarre dreams, endless, timeless dreams, that's all.

Ken wasn't saying anything. Mary was checking her calendar and showing me the date they had left, with the name and the number of the flight, and today's date, with the name and the number of the flight. Then she counted the number of days, with me peeking over her shoulder, and it came out to forty two days. "Six weeks," Mary triumphantly announced for my benefit. I was trying to rehash how it was possible for that amount of time to pass.

Needing an answer, I stopped talking to Mary, went into my room, and began an all out search for my medication, still confident there was some explanation for what had, for me, been but a fitful sleep full of crazy dreams. Just before leaving Berkeley, I had gotten fresh refills on all of my various prescriptions, so I knew the bottles were full when I left and I knew exactly how many bottles there were. All the plastic brown bottles of pills were still full. Whatever I had done during those six weeks, over dosing was apparently not one of them.

All the questions as to what had gone on for the alleged six weeks had, for their answer, dreams and hallucinations. Visions of pyramids and voices, crazy insane voices, speaking to me from every object in my room.

I felt a sick feeling in the pit of my stomach, as though I was no longer in control of my life, if I had ever been in control of my life. I went into the bathroom and sat on the toilet. I put my head into my hands and silently pleaded into my moist palms for an explanation. Amnesia, I thought. But I thought that amnesia was a result of a physical injury to the brain and though my heart wasn't working, my brain surely was.

Finally, I got up the nerve to call a friend of mine in Berkeley, California. He answered the phone as if nothing was wrong and was glad to hear from me.

"Well, you haven't called at all in the last six weeks. I was waiting for you to get settled and then I thought you'd call me. I even wrote you all those letters and you never responded."

"Don't joke around, Jon," I said glumly. "You're joking, right? Tell me you're joking."

"I have better things to joke about," he said. "And so, what happened to you?"

"I only remember that I was having these amazing dreams."

"Not for a month and a half," Jon said, "that's impossible, Daniel."

I laughed. "I would be dead if I had been lying here in my rocking chair unconscious and hallucinating for that long. So what happened to me, Jon? I need a rational explanation."

"Exactly what part of the dreams do you remember?" he asked.

I was trying to recollect any portion of those dreams. "Okay there was Ken," I said. "He, or his voice, seemed to be everywhere, and he kept telling me these stories about pyramids and crystals."

"Crystals?" Jon asked.

"Magic crystals. I don't know. How the hell am I suppose to know. He spread all these crystals about. A boat," I blurted out. "I was on a boat, too."

"What does a boat have to do with anything?"

"It was when I was a kid - my uncle took me aboard this ship."

"So?"

"Something happened on the boat. I can't remember what but it felt like a nightmare. I was just a little kid, so the the images are fuzzy but what I can recall has this weird 'back-in-time' quality ..."

"Shut up, Daniel."

"... as if I'd gone back thousands of years. They were killing someone. I remember that. Someone good was being killed and I was scared. Gosh, I don't know. It's a jumble," I said. Suddenly I knew who the condemned man was, but I couldn't tell Jon. I couldn't even say the words to myself. It didn't make sense and must surely be a dream memory. I changed the subject, "Tell me what you know about the Holy Grail, Jon."

"I know very little, sorry to say."

"How about the person who finds the Holy Grail? What power does that give him?"

Jon paused. "The power over time? I think I heard that somewhere. Time travel."

"Even back to the time of Christ?"

"I suppose ... but who would want to?"

"When I was on this boat as a child, it was as if the boat had spun around some how ..."

"And you landed on Mars? Are you switching to bad science fiction writing, Rogers?

∞ 7 ∞

In the morning I awoke with a start. How much more time had passed? Was it the next morning or was it three months later? I heard a knock on my door. It opened and Mary walked in and sat down on the edge of my bed. "I'm making waffles, if you'd like some."

I followed her back to the kitchen. The door to their bedroom, just off the kitchen, was open and the television was on. Ken, halloed by his freshly washed white hair and beard, was dressed in an orange pullover and white sweat pants and sneakers. He was reclining on the bed, in a blueish light, sipping at a cup of coffee. Mary was making waffles. I said my good mornings.

"Would you mind fixing coffee?" Mary asked. "You didn't make much coffee when we were gone. What did you do, eat out?" She turned her attention back to the waffles in the waffle iron. I nodded.

"You can't afford to eat out. We're paying your room and board, but we are ..."

"Mary," Ken interrupted from his bed. The light on his face had turned into a cold, foggy, blueish light.

"I said, Daniel can't afford to eat out," Mary insisted. "He's on a very limited income. Why do you think I stacked the freezer full of food?"

Ken didn't answer.

I tried to ascertain how the coffee maker worked, trying to conceal the fact that I hadn't even noticed it before.

I neglected to put the plastic top on the coffee pot, as I set the pot in the machine under the filter, where I had decided the coffee would drip out. The result of this neglect was a growing puddle of brown liquid and coffee grounds all over the counter.

"Turn it off, Danny," Mary yelped. "You forgot the top. I can't believe this, I showed you over and over. Just clean it up, okay."

Mary took her plate into the bedroom and closed the door behind her. I grabbed a waffle in hand and went back to my bedroom.

I tried to lie down on the bed with the head propped up to see how long I could remain in that position. I only lasted ten minutes before returning to the safety of my rocking chair. I closed my eyes trying to piece together the past. Pyramids, ships vanishing, space ships going at the speed of light, time machines from other planets.

Restless and searching for reasonable explanations, I went into the living room where Mary's computer and desk were. On the wall nearest the computer were books and Native American artifacts and photos of wonderfully expressive faces. There were books on dolphins, whales, crystals and more dolphins. Crystals and pyramids, planting the crystals, the exact subject matter I had dreamt about, or was it? If only I could remember clearly. I went back to my bedroom and shut the door. Okay, the books would account for the subject matter of the dreams if, that is, I had ever looked at them and I assume I must have. But the books could not account for the time that had passed. And I was damned if there was any magical or cosmic solution to the problem. The plane trip to Texas was real. The car, sailing through the hill country, the woody cuteness of Wimberley, the dog, yes, the dog was real. Mary and Ken leaving for Europe was real.

How could I have eaten meals, gone to the bathroom, let the dog out, given the dog fresh food and water and not remember any of it? Something was wrong, and I didn't know what.

That night I forced myself to watch a video tape of one of Ken's sessions. On the television screen, the woman Ken was working on, lay on a massage table, while an audience looked on. She seemed to be freely associating when Ken asked her to see a color, a light, a symbol, when asked to give an energy a name. And then Ken asked, "Where are you now, inside or outside? Give me the first image that comes to you. Who are you? Who are you, now?" I turned off the TV, refusing to look at what I took to be a form of New Age psychotherapy.

Mary was standing in the open doorway with Polarity at her side, staring at me for I don't know how long. When I finally noticed her, she came in and sat down on the edge of my bed and heaved a sigh. "Danny, the puppy wants to be with you. You did steal his heart, you butthead," she said. "Look, I'm sorry I was such a bitch this morning. I'm still really cranky from the trip. Jet-lag. Sorry." Pause. "You're taking your meds? Feeling okay?"

I nodded and shrugged a response and she pursed her lips at me and shook her head. We sat there in comfortable silence, each knowing that the rhythm of our conversations were often filled with long stretches of silent moments.

Finally, Mary spoke again, "Do you know why you were invited here?" She waited for a response. "Do you want me to give you a hint?"

"I'm here to write about the odd, fantastic and holy."

"No, smart boy. Okay, I'll give you a hint, even though you're in a wretched mood. There's a character in the bible, in the New Testament, that Ken's life, almost down to every detail, has paralleled. I know it's making a stupendous claim, but hear me out."

"So, tell me. Who is it, that Ken's life is like, down to the last detail?"

"No," she said after a pause, "now you will have to find out for yourself, Dano. You'd just make fun of anything I have to say."

"Then answer the question. Why did you and Ken invite me to this wonderland? I thought I was supposed to write a book."

"No, not in the mood you're in now. I won't give you any more hints."

She left and for the next two hours I sat still and tried to reconstruct exactly what it was I had been dreaming about for six weeks. I concluded that furniture is supposed to sit still and look comfortable. It's not suppose to talk, not to me, not to anyone. Why would Ken have come up with the idea to invite me to Texas to live with them? Was he trying to fulfill some biblical prophesy that he thought it was his mission to carry out? What in the hell could he have gotten into his head?

Just before lunch Mary was again standing in the doorway. "I've told Ken you want to hear the story of the Earth Keeper Crystal, okay?" she said. "It's another clue as to why you're here and who's life Ken mirrors. Call it accident or coincidence, if you want. But the details should be interesting to you, as a writer, if nothing else. Come on, you'll enjoy it. Get out of that chair."

∞ **8** ∞

I followed Mary into the living room and sat in a chair facing the fireplace. Mary sat beside Ken on the sofa, and for the longest time we just stared at each other, sipping the hot coffee Mary had passed around. I began to blabber something to the effect that I wasn't the mystical type and that I was indeed having my own problems.

"What problems?" Ken asked, not taking his eyes off of me, as though he knew far more than I knew about what was going on. I didn't know if Mary wanted me to give away the real reason I wanted to hear the story but I felt I had to give out part of it.

"Mary said the story of the Earth Keeper crystal is part of the reason you invited me to Texas." I looked at him, trying to imagine a person who could possibly believe his life in 20th century America was anything like a character's in the bible. What hogwash. But I couldn't see a crackpot in front of me. No, the face of Ken Page was not that of a crackpot. When he looked at you, he was so open and kind, not humble, and certainly not meek, but terribly vulnerable and open. I told him that if there was any special kind of magic that could explain why he and Mary had invited me to Texas, I certainly wanted to know what it was.

"I want you to write a book for me. That's why you were invited," he said.

I kept looking at him, waiting for him to go on.

"And I want it to be called *The Crystal of Arimathæa.*"

I stared at him.

"Do you know what that means?" he asked.

I shook my head. The name was familiar, but for awhile I couldn't place it. Arimathæa. Sounded biblical. Joseph of Arimathæa, of course. Now I remembered that long ago name. Joseph of Arimathæa was a wealthy member of the Sanhedrin who offered his family's tomb for the body of Jesus after the crucifixion. As Christ hung on the cross, he had collected drops of His blood into the same chalice used at the last supper. Then I said, "So tell me, what is the Crystal of Arimathæa?"

"It's what you were dreaming about," Ken answered. "It's the Holy Grail. That's what you're going to be writing about. It will be a book on Joseph of Arimathæa and the Holy Grail."

"Ken, how in the hell do you know what I was dreaming about? I'll tell you one thing. Whatever my dreams were, they were not about the Holy Grail."

He laughed. "Are you sure?"

I thought for a moment. I wasn't sure of anything. I said the title of the book I was suppose to write out loud, 'The Crystal of Arimathæa', as if those words would give me some kind of answer. I did remember crystals being in my nightmares, but what did they have to do with the Holy Grail?

As though he was giving me an answer, Ken spoke and said, "Throughout history, crystals have been special objects of worship. The Holy Grail is a crystal chalice in which the blood of Christ was collected at the time of his death. There are older stories about crystals, but that is the one I want you to write about." He looked down at his lap and paused by a long moment before finishing his thought, "It was said that the blood of the Savior contained all the secrets of God and if you possessed it you could rule the world." He then looked directly at me and said, "One man, Joseph of Arimathæa, collected the blood of the Christ in his Passover chalice and then used it to bring Christianity to Europe. At his death, he gave it to his son and when his son was about to die, he hid it so that the crystal chalice would not fall into the wrong hands. In 1983 the Holy Grail made its last appearance on this planet."

"Are you trying to tell me that the Holy Grail really exists? Are you trying to tell me that you know where the Holy Grail is hidden?"

"I am not trying to tell you anything. You are in Texas to find everything out for yourself. No one can tell you, Daniel. You have to find out for yourself. All I can ask you to do is remember."

"Remember what?"

"Cherry Amethyst is a very beautiful stone. One side of the stone I had in my possession was oval and very smooth. The other side was flat. The entire crystal looked like the eye of an elephant. After I'd had this crystal for about a year, I was asked to go to Kauai with a friend. I was told that I would even be given an opportunity, a window of three days, March fifteenth, sixteenth, and seventeenth, to leave this planet if I chose."

"On Kauai," Ken continued, "I went to visit a close friend who had knowledge of crystals and stones. She told me about an Hindu temple on the island that had an Earth Keeper Crystal. The temple was simply magnificent. It had a striking blue roof and wonderful gardens filled with many ponds and statues. The priests were dressed in the traditional orange Hindu robes. Actual entry to the temple was private and by appointment only, but I didn't know that, and had simply showed up. I went over to the main door of the temple and looked in. One of the priests came over and asked if I would like to join them. There, right in the center of the altar of the temple, was the Earth Keeper Crystal. It was displayed simply,with statues on either side. During the service, men and women sit on different sides, and I sat down on the men's side. The service went on for about half an hour. I watched the others as the priests came by, following their example of what to do with the different colors, herbs and ashes. I couldn't take my eyes off the Earth Keeper. It had one large point, and stood at least four feet tall and two feet across. It probably weighed at least a thousand pounds. I knew that my crystal belonged here. It would be the eye of the Earth Keeper; the same eye that had come to me in a vision in Mexico. After the ceremony, I talked with one of the priests. I showed him the crystal and told him that I needed to give it to them, that it was the most valuable thing I owned. The priest said, 'My teacher doesn't make appointments and very rarely comes out to greet the public'. I said, 'I still need to come. I'll be back at eleven o'clock, on Friday, with your permission, and I'd be honored to present the crystal to your master personally.' It was now Wednesday. I knew the crystal belonged there, I knew it would be accepted." He looked up at me. "Sometimes you just know something and you don't know how it is you know, and it can't be explained in any rational way."

I didn't react. If he was trying to tell me something, I didn't know what it was.

"I woke up on Friday. Friday the seventeenth. I had entered the three day period, the window in which I could leave this earth if I wanted. There was only reason that I really wanted to stay. My life up to this point had been so full. I'd learned a great deal and experienced so much that there was really nothing that I was afraid of. But there was one reason I really wanted to stay here on earth. There was one thing that I didn't understand at all. Relationships. If I chose to stay, relationships between people, like father and son, wife and husband, was what I wanted to understand. No other mission. Nothing else."

"Aren't you being a tad, 'Dear Abby'?" I asked.

"Relationships are what this incarnation is about," Ken said. "Relationships are what it means to be alive. Our lovers mirror our basic issues, helping us to grow." With that, Ken continued his story. "When I said the word relationships it was like this giant light went on and all these bells rang and bugles blew and a voice said, 'You got it. You are now a Gate Keeper.' And I said, 'Gate Keeper?' And there was no answer. I had no idea what gate there was for me to keep."

"Great," I wheezed, "you recognized that 2+2=4. Big enlightenment. Let me make a note of it."

Ken smiled, and went on. "That day I went to visit the far side of the Island. On my way back to town I passed a cemetery. The wind was blowing hard and there was a road sign, a big arrow making a curve, pointing toward the cemetery. The wind was blowing so hard that the sign was shaking. I turned back and went to the cemetery. I knew I was needed.

"I walked around very slowly and felt and released a few spirits. Then I noticed a beautiful statue of Christ on the side of the hill. The statue was about thirty feet high. I walked over and sat next to it. There was nothing else around. All of a sudden the ground started to shake and rumble like something was about to explode. All these souls, these beings were going home, I was going home, you were going home." He stopped. We didn't say anything. He continued. "It was like something that had been waiting to be released for eons of time. It felt very

74

old, thousands of years old, but free. It was ecstasy, like being in the center of a giant beacon light, as it's radiating pure joy."

As I listened to Ken's voice, an image appeared in my mind. Suddenly I could see it so clearly. It was a dirty garbage dump of a little hill. The earth was soaked with blood and horror, and sprouting three, limbless trees. The convict brought his own cross beam, carried on his bruised shoulders. What you couldn't have imagined was how close to the earth they were crucified, to be within reach of the wolves and maggots. Nor could anyone have imagined the screams, as the spikes were driven into the hands and feet. No Roman soldier would have dirtied himself with the task of driving the nails; it was left to one of the prisoners, soon to be crucified himself. No one tells you that at the time of death each prisoner, regular as clockwork, lost his bowels. No one tells you that those who refused to die were blinded by the vultures circling over head, spiraling down only when the prisoner could no longer scream them away. The crucified were refused burial, left on the dead tree to be devoured by the more daring of the predators.

Why was I thinking of the crucifixion in these terms? Why was I even thinking about it at all? I could hear Ken's words in the background.

"When I got to the temple, the service was just ending. About ten people were there. A priest entered in his orange robes and then a second one. I had never seen more than one at a time. A third and a forth priest entered and then the master came into the room.

"He was an older fellow, maybe in his sixties, with a beard and a simple robe. He came in and said, 'How are you?' to all of us. We were all kneeling and everyone around me bowed their heads to the floor. He sat down on the steps, just in front of the crystal, and said, 'I would like to sit down and just relax.' He then started sharing about a trip that was coming up for him, back to India. They were building a new temple in Kauai and he was going to India to see the stones they were carving just for this new temple. Then he said, 'Is there anyone here who would like to share with me?' And I said, 'Yes. I have come a long way. I have something for you. It's the most valuable thing I own and I want to give it to you. It belongs here. It's the eye to the Earth Keeper Crystal. The gate to the Earth Keeper.'

"I stood up, walked over, and I handed him the cherry amethyst crystal. He held it for a moment in his right hand and then looked up and held it up into the light. He said, 'How have you come to be this way?' gesturing at my whole person, with his left hand.

"I answered without hesitation, 'I just am. I'm on my way home.' And he said to the other priests, 'This is what I am talking about. This man represents what it looks like to be on your path.' This wonderful teacher then began sharing with the group stories from his path in life. After he was finished speaking he got up and left as simply as he had entered. I knew I would return for the Sunday service.

"Sunday morning, when I returned to the temple for the service, my crystal was right on the front of the Earth Keeper Crystal, like an eye. The crystal was home, and I knew that everything was the way it should be.

"I knew that my mission was complete. I became profoundly still, and in the stillness I received a message from the Earth Keeper. I was told to let go of my nervous system. I sat there, quietly shaking, feeling the impact of the message all throughout my body. I thought, 'I've had to let go of almost everything. What more will they ask of me?' At that moment, I realized how important it was to let the energy and knowing flow through me, and not hold onto it. So I just let go of everything, anything that I was holding onto as a definition of who Ken Page was or what he was here to do. I let the energy flow and my body felt whole and at peace while my tears of joy covered my cheeks. I felt united with the Earth Keeper and received an awareness of the nervous system and the energetics of body, mind and soul. Nothing would ever remain the same. Change and death was a most beautiful, solemn principle of all life.

"In the Holy Grail legend, it says there are seven secret words. Men throughout history have search for clues about what those words could possibly be. Change and Death are the first two. Time is the third word. God the Father represents Time, which gives birth to all things, Christ, the Son is change, the fruits of our Father's seed, and the Holy Ghost? Who else but Death. Father-Son-Holy Ghost. The Trinity."

I looked up and waited for Ken to continue.

"It was said that the seven words of the Holy Grail were kept secret because, if you were not enlightened, the words could take you into madness. Were these the words that Jesus, after his death, told his disciples and no one else? What power could they possibly have ... to heal ... or bring peace to the world?"

"A man named Paul Tahuti was on that ship when time disappeared, and since then Paul has never been the same. I used to visit him and try to help. We'd met when I was a child and he was in his late teens. His parents were supposed to be very rich, but after what happened to him aboard the U.S.S. Eldridge, they didn't know what to do with him. He kept telling them how the ship had become a time machine and he had gone back in time to Christ's crucifixion. Of course no one believed him. The doctors gave him shock therapy and put him on medication and

kept him in a padded cell. They thought he was hallucinating, but it was the same kind of hallucinations you
were experiencing, Daniel. Tell me if I'm wrong, but
weren't inanimate things speaking to you?"

He waited for me to say something, but I wasn't about
to say anything. How the hell did Ken know all of that?

"Tahuti means *Dweller on the Threshold*," Ken
explained. "Tahuti was said to have lived in the great
Pyramid in Egypt. Sometimes he was portrayed as a dog
or an ape. The Greeks referred to him as *Thoth, Dweller
on the Threshold of Time*." He paused again. I must have
been disappointing him with my obtuseness. "Daniel, may
I ask you a question?"

"Go ahead."

"Tell me what you were doing in 1983, forty years
after the ship vanished. Where was Daniel in 1983, when
the last survivors finally reappeared?"

∞ 9 ∞

In January of nineteen hundred and eighty three, I was diagnosed as a male agoraphobic, suffering from this affliction since the day I was four, or so said the shrinks. Symptoms: not feeling alive, not being able to move. Agoraphobia, for me, meant that I was unable to go anywhere outside of my small room. I was nailed to my chair. Time either stood still or rushed forward and backwards like terrifying great swings of the pendulum. It's like being dead, the only difference being that you don't know you are dead. Two thousand years could very well have passed, and I wouldn't have known.

In 1983, I was a writer, living in Point Reyes Station, a small, arty town in Marin County, northern California. In many ways it resembled a motion picture set more than a real life community. Outside, the ocean and the trees made you feel on permanent vacation. It felt like an escape from reality, an extended stay in a seaside resort. I wrote my pages each day; it was just that I couldn't understand what it was the pages meant. It was as if I was taking dictation but, when I had the nerve to read it, it was all babble.

I had begun writing about an old man who was lost and dying. An old man going senile and losing his mind. He only remembered what happened many years ago when he was a very small child.

That was when I first met Mary. I had just awakened from one of my crucifixion dreams. In my dream the air was thick and heavy and I was lost. I couldn't find my father anywhere. I kept crying out for someone to help me, but the crowd kept yelling, "Crucify Him... Crucify Him." I saw a thin little girl standing in the midst of all these angry, shouting people. I remember her standing there and holding this little dog in her arms. Then I woke up.

Outside, I could see a woman in the distance walking her dog. The heat, hovering above the pavement, for a time, almost obscured her from view. I got up and made coffee and when I peered out the window again she was still coming up the road. I went out and sat on my porch, sipping coffee. When she finally neared my house, she asked if she could have some water for her dog. The dog lapped the water from a paper cup and we talked about dogs and horses and art school and one day buying a horse and one day marrying an artist because an artist would understand her. She decided she would cook us dinner until she saw the inside of my shack. It was the same shack in which Philip K. Dick wrote some of his best science fiction novels on madness, time warps, pain, insanity and the mysteries of the universe. I told her I didn't know what I was writing about and she seemed to understand. I told her I hadn't been alive for the last forty years and this, too, she understood.

I must have spent the next three hours trying to explain to her how all time was kind of squeezed together every time my hero opened his mouth.

"Do you believe in ghosts?" I asked.

"Always."

We talked until dawn, smelling the ocean, the two of us in a shack abandoned to the always of space that surrounded us, that frightened us.

We spent thee days together and then decided to get married. Marriage was all that made sense.

The minister who performed the rite was wearing white tennis shoes and a wrinkled black frock and I didn't hear a word he said. We didn't believe the ceremony had really taken effect. It had been a lark or had it? Mary wasn't sure that a minister could snatch two people in off the street to act as witnesses. It wasn't me who was eccentric, we were eccentric together, not a part of the world that others knew and believed. When we tried to merge into life as it is on this planet, neither of us could do it, we only pretended to do it. She, in many ways, was as different from other people as I was, and so we called it love.

Each morning I would go off to write, a forty minute trip into a town named San Anselmo. We were subsisting on a small inheritance from my grandmother, which was due to run out. And when it did, one of us would have to enter the real world. But until that day, I would write, and she would take her dog for long, long walks by the ocean, transcendent in it's space and beauty and tend our growing flock of strays and injured animals that Mary collected or found on our doorstep.

It was a hilly, beautiful drive into town, and on the drive I would have these wonderful ideas about all the scenes I would compose that day and how they would fit into the whole of my story. But no sooner had the writing started than I fell into the incoherent babble of my central character. He was suppose to be my hero, but he had nothing to do with the plot of the story I was trying to tell. I kept relegating him to the confines of a mental hospital, where his wife had put him, and my plot swirled on without him. It was as if he locked himself away from the story and yet, at the same time, I couldn't stop writing about his senile dementia and its poetry. All he seemed interested in doing was discussing his views and what he could remember of his lost life. He became, for me, a kind of King Lear, mad and helpless, wandering around midst the insane of the world. He ended up speaking to ancient ghosts of his own creation and they would answer him, like some kind of Greek Chorus of babbling fools. It was as if he was living forty years or more each time he made his entrance. He had long, white hair that the nurses pulled back into a pony tail to keep it out of his face and food. He was well-to-do so, unlike the other inmates, he dressed in puffed out, high collared white shirts and trousers. Either it was poetry when he spoke or babble or both.

His intrusions left the book wholly disconnected. I was writing surreal fragments, not a story, but fragments of two stories that I couldn't get to sound coherent. The more I wrote about him, the more I felt there was a force controlling him that he knew nothing about, and what's more, that I knew nothing about. He would say, "I can hold light, the sun, in the palm of my hand."

Everyday, the grass hills would be shimmering with billions of dew drops. The air would be crystal clear, brilliantly clear. But once I got to the coffee shop in San Anselmo, nothing of what I had planned to write was possible to put down on paper. Then, in a library I ran across a book on the life of Jesus. And then the wild thought hit me that it was a Christ figure I had been trying to write about and hadn't realized. I wanted to write about Jesus from an entirely different point of view, and so I started the novel again.

Day by day, however, my spirits continued to deteriorate. The inheritance money was running out and my novel was nowhere near completion. Mary believed in me and knew I could write. She got a job to support us while I struggled along with my writing every day. I felt like a failure, totally responsible for our poverty and so tired and depressed some days that I could barely get out of bed.

One day, I left a note saying that I wanted a divorce. Then I left. I just couldn't face Mary or myself any longer. I thought she was much better off without me, and if I could just get away I might be able to write again and regain my lost self. But things only got worse.

You see, I was very sick at that time, but I didn't know it. My lack of energy, I mistook for depression. Consequently, I never wanted to get out of my chair. I didn't know I had heart problems until I walked into a doctor's office, no longer able to breathe, and they stuck me in the hospital.

Two weeks later I was moved from the Intensive Care Unit at Alta Bates Hospital into my own room and that's when I saw her again.

She was sitting in the corner of my room, waiting for me to wake up. She sat there and slept there on a portable bed, each day and night for the next week, never leaving my bedside.

∞ 10 ∞

Once a Frisbee has been damaged by dog teeth, it acquires magical properties. Once thrown, the fang-marked Frisbee does what the thrower did not expect it to do. It rises inches from the ground and arches into the air only to curve in a new direction, a decision as if made by the plastic disk itself.

I am not sure how a dog, poised waiting for the plastic disk to curve towards his mouth, could account for these unexpected mid-air corrections. Ken was the better of the Frisbee tossers, able to throw it straight or curve it in any direction he decided it should fly. He had just thrown the red spinning disc, skimming along a foot off the ground, and Polarity stood his ground as it landed in his mouth. Mary twirled away in disgust that his throw had been so perfect. I applauded.

"Why can't I do that?" she cried as Polarity came trotting to her, not wanting to release his hold on the Frisbee, but desperately wanting Mary to throw it. Mary reached for it, Polarity pulled it away. When Mary didn't reach for it, Polarity begged her to take it, only to pull it away at the last instant. Finally, Mary, tired of waiting, made a grab for it and handed it to me. My throw was superb. At the last instant, the red disc rose into the air so that Polarity was forced to leave the ground, catching the disc solidly in mid-air.

"Good throw," Mary called. Ken nodded. I shrugged, having no idea how I had performed the feat. Polarity came trotting back, always to Mary, always ambivalent; the

84

need to have the Frisbee thrown greater than his need to keep it for himself. This time Polarity shoved the disc hard against Mary's knees. Mary only took hold of it once the dog had appropriately begged and pleaded. At last she grabbed it and ran over to Ken, pressing her body against his and kissing him on the lips before handing him the Frisbee. Polarity was already trotting twenty yards downfield, now and then looking back in order to see if the Frisbee had been thrown.

This time Ken arched it high over a tree branch and the dog flew, skidding in the leaves and raising a cloud of dust. He leaped for the prize and trapped the Frisbee between his front feet instead of catching it in his mouth.

"Cat catch," I called.

"Bird throw," Ken called.

"Mr. P., come here," Mary ordered.

Choking on the dust he's sucked into his mouth, Polarity dropped the Frisbee, cleared his throat, picked it up, and once again delivered it to Mary. This time he offered his Frisbee almost eagerly, insisting she take it before he had to dissolve into his instinctual ambiguity.

Mary let fly before the young dog was half way to where our property ended and the trees began. This time he failed to look behind himself and the disc sailed over his head; the confused dog not knowing which way to go.

"Look up. Up. Up," Ken called.

"He doesn't know what 'up' means," Mary corrected with a laugh. Then she whispered something to Ken which I wasn't suppose to hear. All I could think about was that they wanted to dash into the house to make love, but I also knew that I was imagining it.

Mary growled, shoved the Frisbee into Ken's white shirt, and dashed towards the house to answer a phone that was ringing. The dog froze, staring after.

Ken was already threatening to take his mind off the unexpected tragedy by launching the disc high into the air so that once again the dog didn't have to move a step in order to catch it. Even after he caught it, he was still staring at the front door of the house.

"How do you do that?" asked I.

"Do what?"

"Get it to go straight when you want it to."

"You don't' have to use any muscle. Watch, you can throw it with your breath."

Polarity was sitting at Ken's feet, holding the Frisbee in his mouth. Finally, he dropped it on the grass as if the decision was too much for him, and, doing his sheep dog crawl, crept away.

I looked at him, "Private property was never a decision we made. We were born to it," I said, commenting on the dog and his adamant ownership of the Frisbee.

"Breathe out as you throw it. Empty yourself and once you are empty of breath, you have all the power you need. Ghandi said that," Ken instructed.

"Since when do you metaphysical types ever try to empty yourselves," I said. "All I hear you doing is empowering yourselves with love and light."

"Ghandi was certainly greatly empowered and empty at the same time."

"And if you empty yourself and you still don't get what you want? You want to be a saint without the pain?"

The puppy was offering his Frisbee to me and was tired of waiting for me to take it.

"The trick," Ken said, "is to want, with all your heart, what you get, not what you ask for."

I had noticed his use of the word, heart. "Easy to say when you have what you want."

"And what do you want, Daniel?"

I took the Frisbee and threw it as hard as I could. It curved far out into the tree lined avenue. Polarity made a dash towards the street, without checking first to see if there were any cars approaching.

"Besides love and my health, I can't think of much," I answered him.

"Do you want Mary back?" he asked, clapping his hands for the dog to get out of the street. "You didn't exhale, you took the high inhale," he laughed and asked me again, "Do you want her back?"

I didn't answer. Obedient dog gives Frisbee obediently to Ken and Ken hands it to me.

"Do it again, only this time exhale deeply and at the bottom of the deep exhale, let go of the Frisbee."

I did as he told me and added, "I fell in love with the way Mary talks to animals."

"No," he corrected, "deep exhale. That wasn't even a shallow exhale. Force it down. Hard! Not quick, just hard. There's a difference between quick and hard."

I did 'hard business' several times until I could exhale and time the exhalation with the release of the Frisbee. When I was able at last to hit the release and breath together, the plastic disc seemed to take off and sail straight and far, yet I wasn't conscious of throwing it with any additional muscle. It appeared to be more a matter of smoothness of movement and timing that made the Frisbee soar.

"The life force is all there is," Ken said, "All energy is in the breath. The soul is the breath." The dog was waiting. He stood poised, crept forward, then froze again, never losing his concentration. "All the body knows of time is the breath and the heart beat. When you can overcome that fear of being out of breath, time moves into another dimension." He handed me the Frisbee and told me to try again. "The inhale is automatic, not the exhale. Throw it with your wrist not your arm or shoulder. The spinning will keep it in the air, rather than force. You see, things are never what they seem."

The dog had slowly been creeping ever closer until he crouched ten feet from where we were standing.

"Polarity won't see the Frisbee if you throw it too high," Ken said. "His idea of time and space doesn't include anything higher than a few feet over his head. Everything higher than that, Polarity considers impossible. That's your problem, too. Any idea other than the rational is inconceivable to you."

"And without the rational, where do we end up?"

Ken took the Frisbee and threw it high into the air. Polarity had no idea it had been thrown because he couldn't see it until it landed six inches from his nose.

"That's why we call it the metaphysical. For Polarity, anything over his head, is nothing that his physical senses experience. For Polarity 'up' is metaphysical hogwash, not supported by empirical fact."

"If everything is true, you'd go mad."

Ken laughed. "No one said enlightenment was easy."

Polarity was sitting in front of Ken, offering up the Frisbee. Ken took it and handed it to me. "When you think you have exhaled, you haven't even begun. You're like the puppy. He needs to hold onto the Frisbee, but if he holds onto it, he can't play. Exhale, Daniel, and then you can play. So why can't you breathe? You're holding on. Exhale, Daniel."

I was feeling light headed, but I was used to that. I was also feeling faint, but I knew if I waited the dizziness would soon pass. I was accustomed to the chest pains and alone they would not have caused me unnecessary concern yet, combined with the other symptoms, I knew something was wrong. I had wanted to ask him if the breath was the fourth of the secret words.

Maybe the secret is in holding the breath until the first panic, that tells you you're out of air, passes. But the body is not out of air and the panic ceases and you realize there is now a special kind of breath you are breathing. The light breath. You have gone past the 'small death'. You are now breathing the light breath.

No sooner had I thrown the Frisbee, than I toppled over onto the grass, head down as if bowing deeply. I couldn't see anything, but I could hear Ken calling for Mary. I could hear the dog's panting and wondered if he was breathing correctly. I could hear Mary rushing out of the house, and asking, "What's wrong?" I couldn't any longer catch my breath, like all those times I couldn't catch my breath when Mary and I were making love. Her hand was touching me, her voice at my ear, "What's wrong, Danny? Ken, go. Call an ambulance, now."

Then I remembered a dog beside a pyramid, hidden in the Yucatan, and I was trying to throw the Frisbee to that dog, or was it the same dog that was now licking my face, as I lay on the grass.

∞ 11 ∞

A blinding white ceiling, spot lights embedded in the white ceiling. "You're okay," said a nurse looking down at me and patting my shoulder gently.

The doctor's face had replaced the face of the nurse. "How do you feel, Mr. Rogers?"

"Lousy..."

"You're dehydrated."

Squeezing a rubber ball that tightened the thick, cool wrapping on my arm, he stared over my head at the mercury scale.

"We think you might have had a small episode," said the doctor. "You should drink more water. We're going to do a few tests, then you can go home."

"I'm a psychiatrist," another voice said. "Do you feel well enough to talk. Excuse me, would everyone kindly leave the room."

I thought I heard Mary's voice in the hallway. I didn't want her to leave. The shrink smiled as if I was simply exaggerating my pain.

"I'm going mad," I said.

"You're on a lot of medication. Why do you say you're going mad? What are you feeling?" he asked.

"Because I am," I whispered.

"What does the word mad mean to you?"

Again I began the story of my trip to Texas, putting particular stress on the fact that there was no way six weeks could have gone past as fast as they did, or at least, not without my knowing it.

"Okay, I know I didn't take my pills," I winced, trying to breathe.

"Anyone, who has come as close to death as you did with your heart problem, is bound to go through a reactive depression which is why they put you on those anti-depressants in the first place. You see, there are explanations for everything. You have several survival issues you are trying to deal with, meanwhile I'll give you a prescription for more medication."

"I'm not going to take your pills, Doctor," I whispered. "You can go to hell with your pills."

"Excuse me?"

"Hell, you know. Hades, perdition, the bottomless pit, the inferno."

"I'm afraid you don't have a choice, Mr. Rogers."

"Screw your pills and your idea of what a choice is..."

"Stop taking the anti-depressants if you must, but don't stop taking your heart pills."

"There's a Mr. Page here to see you," interrupted a nurse and I felt, rather than saw, the doctor backing out of the room, saying that he would check with me later.

"Couldn't find a place to park in the shade." I saw Ken's face staring down at me, smiling down at me, his white beard always so perfectly trimmed. "Mary and the pup are playing Frisbee in the parking lot." A long silence.

He pulled up a chair and sat down. "You were asking me about the key to the Holy Grail." He smiled, and then sat there. It seemed like years ago that I had asked such a question. "Well, are you going to write that book for me?"

"I'm not really very big on biblical scholarship," I said.

"Who says you have to be," he said. "You already know all there is to know."

"Great," I said. "Good thing I know it. Always wanted to know everything in the universe. Like Faust. Maybe I'm the reincarnation of Faust. He too wanted to know every-thing there was. He even wanted to know how to square a circle. I wonder if he ever found out. Hey, I'm not just some guy in the New Testament, I was a character in Goethe's poetry, Mr. Page."

"You really believe that time is your obedient little dog on your own special leash, heeling at your side, sitting when you stop, coming when you call." He laughed, sitting there as if he had all the time in the world.

"Hardly," I said, feeling somewhat better, at least able to catch my breath. "For me, time isn't even a domestic animal, and certainly not house broken."

"Better get used to time as a dog who is not on your linear leash," he said. "You see, I've got this notion in my head that multidimensional time is a process we all know quite well. In this life we're introduced to it in our dreams. Have you ever thought about what time is like in your dreams? It's not the same as when you're awake."

"I'd rather not talk about the cosmic, if you don't mind," I said. "That Frisbee Breath almost did me in."

"I was thinking about your first six weeks in Texas and how linear time went awry for you. You see, I believe that dreams are higher dimensions of a reality just as true and real as our everyday life."

"You mean that, don't you?" I said. "Do you know the secret of the Holy Grail? If you know the secret you, Ken Page, could rule the world."

Again, his open and gentle smile. "And what if I already rule the world?' he said.

"If you do, then I have indeed underestimated you. No wonder Mary fell in love with you."

"You decide, Daniel. Here's a clue. In his later life, when Joseph of Arimathæa's son saw a vision of Christ, he saw Christ's face as a flaming red ball of fire."

I recalled the red glass ball of fire that had been speaking to me in my bedroom. He was either reading my mind or he was taking a wild guess.

"Like I said, time is not our little freshly washed dog, trotting by our side. Tell me, how did human kind get to the state where we could write off, could dismiss, one third of our lives, our sleep and dream time? How, as a civilization, could we develop such a notion? The only reason you think you're mad is that your dog has refused to come when you call."

"I tried, once upon a time, to write a novel," I said. "and I gave it up because I couldn't understand my hero who, come to think of it, looked and talked a great deal like you. I thought my hero was a crazy old man."

"Dreams and the imagination are at the core of time, though today no one understands that. Today, we divide the world into categories. We separate time from the creative imagination. The imagination is a multidimensional, timeless use of time. In dreams just like in the imagination, there is no time." There was a long pause.

"See," I laughed. "My hero would say things like that, and I'd say to myself, 'What the hell does that mean?'"

"Think about it. Is time only the second hand circling the numbers on your wrist watch? Is that what you've been taught? That time is how often the sun rises and falls, the days you mark off on some calendar? What a silly idea. Come up with something better."

"My dog just broke away," I said, "and is dashing across an open field."

"Good," Ken said. "It's about time. Excuse the pun."

We sat there not talking, not looking at each other. I was trying, in my head, to imagine dreams being as real as waking life, but as yet, I couldn't quite conceive of it. I didn't know what the problem was, but I still relegated dreams to a lower level of reality. For me, laundromats were what was real. What if dreams were as real and true as my waking life? Could I ever reach a point when I really believed that?

"I, too, was afraid of death," he said.

"Who said I'm afraid of death?" I asked. "What does that have to do with anything?"

"Your fear of death is why you can't make the leap, Daniel. Why you're stuck wanting to believe me, but your fear stops you."

"What does fear of dying have to do with accepting my dreams as real experiences?"

"Death is not only loosing the dog, but never being able to get him back on the leash. Dying is never again getting time to obey."

"You're loosing me."

"Death is the fear of losing whatever tiny bit of control you ever thought you possessed. Just like your dreams are not under your control, neither is death. The fear of death is the fear of losing control and never getting it back. We're all afraid, terrified of letting go."

"So, that's the secret of the Holy Grail?"

"A few years ago, a terrible famine hit Egypt and most of the African continent and thousands were dying, men, women and children. I saw the pictures on the television and for nights I wasn't able to go to sleep. I might be able to help others, others who were but mirrors of myself, a part of the same energy. I heard a voice and it was saying to me, 'There are dying people who are going to get lost. Many of them will be children, and they are going to be hungry and afraid. Many will have difficulty finding the Light because their families wish so desperately to hold onto them, or they were confused, or in great pain.' This message moved me greatly as I had, in a past life, left my children and they were forced to grow up without me. In this life, I was being forced to do the same, so that for me children were everywhere.

"At that time, I also believed in polarities. There was good and bad, victims and saviors, living and dead. That distorted belief forced me to retire from my healing practice. I begun to work part-time in a horse stable. I figured, 'Well, so much for my career.' I needed to get myself straightened out. I would get up very early in the morning and feed all the horses. Then I would go inside, put my suit on and go to work at my regular job. I returned home about one thirty in the afternoon, changed clothes, and went out again to clean the stalls and feed the animals. Now I knew exactly what shit I was shoveling. The shit was all very real, very tangible to my senses. It turned out to be the best therapy I could have gotten."

He waited for me to say something and then continued with his story, "About that time, the mother of someone I worked with was quite ill. She was going to pass away, and she was in a coma in the hospital. My friend asked me if I could go over and see her, which I did. I usually set up ideomotor responses with my clients, using the fingers of one hand as signals for yes and no. In this particular case we were able to set up her ideomotor responses, even though she was in a coma, by using her toes. Since she was in a coma, however, and I could not be sure of her level of subconscious awareness, I went ahead and pulled the energy off her, took it on myself and then released it. It was a negativity.

"I felt that her primary concern was what was going to happen to her family at Christmas. She had always held the family together. What would happen when she was gone? I worked with her awhile longer, until I felt her peace and knew she was calm. Death can be looked at two ways. One is that you, as an individual, die alone. The second way is that everyone else in the world is gone except you and you are trapped in the void.

"Her children said they would call if they needed me and I left for the day to go back to the barn. When I got done with my chores, about seven o'clock that evening, I got a call and they asked me to come back. When I got there, the room was full of people and I knew for sure it was getting close to the time for her to pass on. I sat beside her, touching her head with one hand and her arm with the other. The monitors were behind me and I was talking to her, taking her into a meditation, having her explore other worlds, other realities, like a bird. I explained to her that it was okay to let go, that her family and I were holding the space for her and that she need not be afraid. Then I said, 'Now, I want you to stop taking the physical breath and take the Light Breath.' Just as I said this, her heart monitor flat lined and she passed on.

"At that moment, the Light came down. This was a person who was scheduled to pass on and the Light, the Source, came down for her. At that moment, I was able to hold that space for a split second and the Light went all over the planet. It was the most beautiful, amazing, electric experience. Everyone in the room felt what happened and their perceptions shifted. Time had stood still for them and they knew it.

"As I was leaving, they asked me to come back in a day or so just to talk to the group and I did that. Each of them stood up and talked about their experience that night and how it changed their life, how they felt God.

"And those souls in Egypt, Ken? What happened to them? Are you saying you saved them all in that one moment of Light?"

"Don't fall into the trap. I am not talking about myself, Ken Page, as the savior of millions of souls. Even my ego is not that big." He hesitated before going on, "There was a second breath. A special being held the consciousness and her name was Cindy. She was thirty-four years old and dying of old age. Cindy was a horse. She had been in my cousin's family for a long time. When her day came, I found her lying down in her paddock and she could not get up. I tried to help her but she was too weak. Since it had been raining and was muddy, I got blankets underneath her and then I waited, holding her head in my lap. A couple hours later, as I cradled and stroked her beautiful chestnut head, she died. She took a breath and passed into the Light. And when she did that, to my surprise it happened again. The Light shone out all over the planet and then I realized that horse consciousness is very, very powerful indeed. The Light went out from this little muddy paddock. It's not just me. We all have this power. We live a lifetime in order to learn how to breathe, yet only those close to death can breathe like that. The samurai trains his whole life to take his last breath every instant of every day. Tell me why?"

"Why?"

"Because he must let go of the polarities, release the illusion of the self into the reality of the whole. Can you let go of your nervous system, your brain, your sexual organs? What makes you different from the whole, the oneness? That is the question the samurai, moment by moment, must ask himself.

"The third breath was with my grandfather. He would often tell me stories. He was Catholic and very religious. When he was about eighty-nine his health was extremely poor. He'd talk in his sleep about angels coming and he would fly with them and talk to them. I told him I'd be with him when he passed on.

"Then the day came when they called me. He'd gone into a coma during the night. And so that Saturday morning, as I held him in my arms and I told him it was okay to take his last breath, he did.

"The conclusion I came to, about myself, after these experiences, was that I was a gate. The more connected I was to my spiritual self, the more Source flowed through me and I became a gate to other worlds, other realities, and other dimensions. After death the wind will be your breath, hovering over your grave. Everything on this planet is alive. The Native Americans know that. Many of us have yet to learn that. The blood runs as a river. We are all interconnected, one breath away from salvation. The Frisbee sails into the air and it doesn't stop."

"I am not a savior. I don't want to be enlightened. I don't want to be a gate," I said. "I don't want to save millions of souls, only my own."

"It isn't your choice. You have created for yourself all there is. And you have done it on thousands of different levels, which you can't begin to understand."

"Do you want me to take the last breath. I assure you, I would love to take the last breath, like the horse did, like that woman in the hospital did. But when I do, no souls in Egypt will ever know the difference."

"Let go of your personal ego, let go of your existence in linear time and space. Maybe truth and fiction are not different. Here and there doesn't matter. We divide reality into polarities only so that we can return the polarities to their original state of wholeness and completion."

"Is this what you call healing?" I asked turning away.

"Everything that happens to you, I call healing. Mary, you and I are mirroring each other. Showing us how we need to heal ourselves, what we most need to know. In that way we are healing and teaching each other. You are a mirror. Therefore, you are part of a greater whole, not a mere individual bag of flesh and bones. You are trying to remember that wholeness. Past, present and future are now and forever interconnected in ways we can't imagine, staring at our calendars the way we foolishly do."

The nurse had come in to take some more blood and feed the hungry vampire in the basement. The nurse left, blood and all.

"What do you mean that we're all interconnected? What I do affects no one in Egypt, I assure you."

"Do you realize how the world would change if say, in the gospels, Peter had not denied Christ three times? When asked by the Romans if he was not a friend of that man who called himself the Messiah, what if Peter had overcome his fear of death and answered, 'I am his friend.' What would have happened then? What would have been the effect on history?"

"I have no idea."

"Peter's greater faith couldn't have existed in a vacuum. The other disciples would have been affected by Peter's willingness to die, even if only to a small degree. Perhaps just enough to make Judas hold off for a day, a week, a year, no longer certain that betraying Christ was worth the forty pieces of silver. Maybe Judas went up to the Romans and was about to open his mouth and say, 'I'll take you to Him.' but at the last moment remembered Peter with all of his weaknesses and all of his courage and faith, and suddenly, Judas couldn't do it. Say it was a month, a year before Judas finally offered the Romans his deal and betrayed Christ. What if Jesus lived for another month or even performed one more miracle, uttered one more parable, what would have been the effect? Perhaps another Roman would have been converted to Christianity five minutes earlier, five days earlier and nineteen hundred years later Adolph Hitler came into power but couldn't get it together to persecute the Jews or at the last instant, the atom bomb was not dropped on Hiroshima, and nuclear technology did not have the stage on which to prove how horrifying it could be, and the theory remained only a test in the laboratory, and all because Peter said, 'I am His friend.' Change one leaf of the past and history will be rewritten in ways no one can imagine."

∞ **12** ∞

A nurse had delivered a no-salt, no-flavor lunch. Ken was still talking, but I had gotten no closer to any secrets of the Holy Grail.

"I had yet another chance to see if I was looking at time through Death's eyes, because if I was still believing in time as my pet golden retriever, I couldn't have understood what I know now."

"You mean that dreams are other dimensions of time? I got it. You're trying to convince me that during my first six weeks here, I was in another dimension, right? I don't buy it, Ken."

"Explain it to me then," He said, staring at me. "I don't think you can."

"Amnesia. that would explain it, wouldn't it?"

"Only if you fell and hit your head. You'd love the explanation to be amnesia, wouldn't you? So explain this. It was raining as I started out to my car around eight thirty in the evening, and kind of chilly. I was at the Nut Tree, a restaurant in Napa County, for a business meeting. The meeting was over and I had just bought some beautiful crystals in their gift shop before heading home. I took the crystals and zipped them into my coat so that the bags would not get wet and let the crystals drop out. My car was on the other side of the parking lot.

"As I put the crystals against my heart and ran to my car, I could feel a change, a connection. When I got to the car and took the crystals out, I felt very heavy, very sober.

It felt like I was to go to war and fight something so large, so big that it could kill me. And if I didn't do it, I would die and have to come back and try again.

"I drove home through the Napa Valley area on the Silverado Trail. At this time it was still raining and about eleven o'clock. Silverado is a two way lane, way out in the country. There's nothing but vineyards. A beautiful area, probably one of the most beautiful areas in the whole world. The trees, the vineyards, the quiet lanes. But this night, there was a storm and it was raining very hard. I had taken one of the crystals out of the bag and I was holding it in my right hand. It had seven sides, one point with a ball shape on the opposite end. I was also holding, in my left hand, a crystal that Paul had given me. Both crystals were in the top part of my hands, pointing towards each other, and my palm was resting on the top of the steering wheel. I was listening to the radio and I felt kind of tired. It had been a long day.

"I came upon a long stretch of the road and I could see a car coming towards me, its lights were bright. Then, all of a sudden, another car passed him coming towards me in my lane and we were going to collide. I hit my brakes and as I did, my car slid sideways. His headlights filled my window. The impact would be any moment, the car was only feet away. Then everything went black. My dog of time had broken loose from his leash. Had twenty minutes past? Or was it just a moment?

"When I was conscious of my surroundings again, I found myself slowly coasting down the road in my lane. I looked all around for the other cars. In my rear view mirror only one set of red tail lights were going away. I pulled the car over and sat there. If you were to tell me it was the year 3000, I would have believed you. Maybe I was on my own little vanishing boat. Like a dream, a piece of my consciousness, that was actually functioning in another dimension, came into me. Everything that I knew, everything that I understood, was about to change for me. Everything that I owned, I loved, I worked with, I saw, I felt, was going to change. It was overwhelming."

I looked away.

"You never told me what your nightmares were about, Daniel."

"They were about you," I said.

"Maybe they were trying to tell you something."

"In my dreams, you were trying to drive me crazy. That's what you were trying to do."

"Why would I want to do that?"

"I wish I knew."

"I was trying to keep you alive, Daniel."

"Thanks, but no thanks."

"You remember the eye, floating in ..."

"Get out of here," I screamed. "And don't come back. Do you hear me? Don't come back. You can take all your nutty ideas and go to hell with them."

Ken left the room and I was alone. In the middle of the night, I experienced the terror of not having anything to think about.

∞ 13 ∞

Before the sun had risen, I pressed the button for the nurse and looked around for my clothes. I had to sit back down to catch my breath, hoping that my spell was due to the fact I had gotten out of bed too quickly. I took three deep breaths.

The nurse was standing in the doorway, "May I help you, Mr. Rogers?"

"I need to check out," I said, "before 2+2 no longer equals four." It was not a request, it was a declarative sentence, a simple, straight forward fact. I had concluded there were not enough simple, straight forward facts in my life, up to this point.

"Mr. Rogers, the doctor has a few tests scheduled for later today."

"My mind is what's wrong with me," I said trying to sit up but taking it far more slowly this time. "I was right when I ran away from my wife the first time. Why in hell did I come back?"

"You had better stay in bed. Lie down."

"I said I'm leaving this joint. I've had it with being sick. I went through seven hours of surgery and I didn't exactly get all better. The doctors have had their chance." Again I tried to stand up, and again I sat back down.

"You're not leaving here," she insisted.

"That's what you think. My ex-wife is married to a lunatic," I said. "Just give me a chance to catch my breath and I'm out of here."

"Where do you think you're going in your condition?" the nurse said defiantly, both hands on her hips.

"Anywhere but here. No more knives, no more pills. No more miracles. Keep them for someone who believes in your cut and sew version of voodoo."

Again I tried to stand up, this time forcing myself to ignore what my body was telling me, and my body was sending the message loud and clear that I was going to, at best, faint. The nurse came up and held my hand to steady me as I looked around for my clothes. "Which way is Egypt?" I quipped and suddenly I was laughing, wailing with gales of belly laughter.

"Mr. Rogers, you are not leaving this hospital." She gently eased me back down onto the edge of the bed. "I'll have to call the doctor."

"This is a free country. So, you think we're in Nazi Germany, do you? Call Herr Doktor." Again I started to get up, but again, with cool, white hands on my shoulders, she insisted I stay down. Now it was her turn to press the red button in order to summon help.

"That's not going to do you any good," I said and pushed her away, stumbling blindly towards the closet, hoping that if I moved around a tad I would get used to the dizziness. For whatever reason, I didn't give a damn about my heart or the pain or if I died here on the spot. Maybe it didn't matter because I wasn't sure it was real in the first place; I wasn't sure that the entire state of Texas wasn't a dream. If I was to die, right now, I was reasonably sure I would wake up again back at Mary's with that damn dog on my lap. And the dog would be giving me dog kisses, wet dog kisses and Mary would be lecturing me about wasting money in this quack hospital. So what if I had a heart attack, there was no way in hell the gods would allow me to get off that easily.

Usually, I was shy about how I looked, especially in front of the opposite sex since congestive heart failure had bloated my stomach, but boldly I released the strings of my green paper pajamas and stood, ass naked, looking for my shirt and underwear in the small closet.

Just then a male attendant appeared in the doorway. He was black and looked like a defensive tackle for the Dallas Cowboys. He had a stern look on his face.

"Please," ordered the nurse, "help Mr. Rogers back into his bed."

"It's a free country," I repeated. Then I felt a hand on my shoulder. I spoke to him very confidentially. "Do you know, I spoke to a man yesterday who saved all of the African continent."

"Come on buddy. Let's lie ye old body down."

"Let's lie ye old body down?' I said, resenting the fact that I was naked while this minor dispute was taking place. "That's good. I like that." The hand on my shoulder grew more insistent, consistently applying the encouragement needed for me to 'lie me old body down'.

"I'll call Anwar Sadat. I'll call Nelson Mandela," I said. "I'll tell them I'm being kept here against my politically incorrect will." I tried to jerk my shoulder away from his grip and fell, ass first, to the cool, always clean floor.

The attendant was smiling down at me. Then he offered me a hand. I saw the nurse on the phone asking for my doctor "stat". If I only had my clothes, this whole episode would not have been so humiliating.

"I'm leaving here," I said crawling towards the bed so that I would have something to hold onto while I attempted, at least, to get to my knees. But even holding onto the bed didn't help me get up.

Now it was the doctor's turn to smile down at me from the doorway. Unlike the others, he was relaxed, well dressed and trying to appear professional. Unlike me, he had all of his clothes on which gave him an advantage.

"What's the problem here?" he said.

"Mr. Rogers wants to leave us," said the nurse.

"You don't like the food?" he said, the smile having left his face for a distinguished pout.

"I have better things to do," I said. "I've been in hospitals and it's my experience that I don't leave hospitals feeling any better than when I came in. As a matter of fact, I've noticed that most of the time I feel worse. You save my life only to make me feel lousy. Bad deal."

"What do you think you're going to do if you leave in your present condition?" said the doctor, smiling warmly.

"You can't keep me here against my will."

"No, I can't, but I strongly advise against it," the doctor responded, and then turning to leave he addressed my nurse with, "Let him go. He'll be back. Give him my home phone number. 911."

That was not the answer I expected. Then I looked at the nurse. "Would you kindly get me my clothes and a wheel chair and a taxi cab. 911, very funny."

The attendant also left and the nurse watched me struggling into my clothes. She summoned a wheel chair while I called for a taxi cab and told them it was an 'airport call'. Then the nurse wheeled me to the elevators and through the brown lobby out into the bright sunlight, me whistling 'Peg-O-My Heart'.

The taxi cab was waiting at the curb, the driver sitting in the car smoking and reading a racing form. I struggled into the cab without the drivers help, and we drove wordlessly to the airport. I was half way to Austin before realizing that no one at the hospital had asked me to sign any discharge papers or pay a penny. Ken must have taken responsibility for the bill.

At the airport, a wheelchair was summoned before I got out of the back seat of the taxi and I was wheeled to the airline ticket counter. I flashed them a credit card, was wheeled to gate fourteen and aboard the aircraft.

I was already feeling better once I was seated near a window, just like I'd been on my way to Texas. Maybe I would never return to Texas, I thought, trying to catch my breath. Climbing into my seat had worn me out, so when the plane was in the air, I told the stewardess I did not want a drink, that I was drunk enough on my own extravagant, self pity. Did I really have reason to believe that returning to Berkeley would answer any of my questions? What did I think I was gaining by all this melodrama? Mary's tears if I died?

Once the plane was in the air I consoled myself with the idea that what I was really doing was leaving Texas, once and for all. I was going where the sane people of the world were situated. Then I dosed off and the image of my father appeared to me in my dreams.

My father had me in his arms, my face hidden in his white beard, dripping with his sweat and his anger. I could hear pieces of wood dropping to the hard earth or stone and clay, earth that was neither up hill nor down hill, and you couldn't call it flat, because it took too much effort to traverse. I could hear yelling and commands being cried out and the words, 'This is the place.' And for the first time, my father was speaking to me and telling me that my sister was alive only because of this man they were about to crucify. It wasn't the first time I had heard that word. I had heard stories about that word. And I remembered a day when my father and mother had been so sad and then so happy. My sister had been locked away from the rest of the family, as if she was dead. When she came out there was much rejoicing, and a male voice had said that men who do things like He has done, will be crucified; the worst death the Romans were able to imagine.

I awoke as if from a nightmare, unable to make any sense at all out of that dream, but at least I was able to remember it. In my dream, a man had been carrying me in his arms and he was my father, but not my father in this life. It had been someone else familiar to me, but the dream had obscured who he was.

Once the plane landed, I made my way into the Oakland terminal, the same terminal I had left from. Why had I ever left? The answer, if indeed it was an answer, was standing before me, bright eyed and freshly bathed and trimmed as ever. Ken.

"Fancy meeting you here," I said.

"Have a seat." He indicated the wheelchair. "Mary told me you were fond of running away. I know that feeling well myself. I'm a master at running. And besides that, the hospital called."

The Hertz Rent-A-Car was parked at the curb. I remember riding in the car like a tourist, watching the familiar scenery of Oakland. I had no idea where he was taking me and I didn't ask. He was beginning yet another one of his stories. I wondered if he was about to reveal the fifth of the secret words. Change, Death, Time, Breath.

"The year was 1983," he said once we'd made our way onto the freeway, as if we were continuing our conversation and had only been interrupted by one of those all knowing transcendent silences. Another crystal chalice and I'll puke, I thought impatiently.

"I owned several resorts in Clear Lake and these were exceptionally tough times for me."

Yeah, sounds like another crystal story, I thought.

"We'd gone through heavy flooding in the last two years and I'd been trying to recover." Then Ken looked straight at me and said, "In 1983 you ran away from Mary because you refused to remember. Close your eyes, Daniel. What was it you were running away from? Move there now. Are you inside or outside?"

I didn't answer.

"Are you male or female?"

I was trying to remember something that happened long, long ago. I was inside with no way, no way at all, of knowing whether I was male or . . . It was because I was so young, lying there on my uncle's bed pretending to be asleep and then before I knew it, I was aboard a ship. I wasn't supposed to be there either, just like I wasn't suppose to be at the crucifixion. Why was I having all these weird thoughts?

"Listen to me," Ken was saying, "and look straight ahead. What do you see?"

"Ghosts. I see ghosts," I said. "They are trying to be human and not able to be human. They're frozen in this greenish light. Why can't they move?"

"They were disappearing," Ken answered, "that explains the green light, why they can't move."

"I don't want to do this anymore," I whispered.

"It was just like when you first arrived in Texas and you thought the medication was giving you dreams. It was the fact that you didn't want to remember. Daniel, you were replaying what happened to you aboard that ship. How old were you?"

"Four," I said.

"Is anyone with you?"

"My uncle," I said. I could see him clearly. "He's frightened. He can't move, he's trying . . . I must be making this up. It was just a dream."

"The year was 1983. You were, at the same instant, both in 1943 and 1983. Your uncle is holding you. What do you hear?"

"The humming."

"What humming?" Ken asked.

"I don't know."

"What happened after you heard the humming?"

"I don't know . . . I woke up."

"Where?"

"I don't know. The image I keep seeing in my mind is the day I met Mary."

"What year was it?" Ken continued.

"I was trying really hard to wake up, is how it felt, how I remember it," I answered.

"It was forty years later," Ken told me.

"No, you're crazy."

"You were four years old in 1943 and Mary told me it was 1983 when you met. She said you couldn't account for all the time in between. Could you, Daniel? How much of your life was missing?"

"I was sick. I was sick a lot."

"Understand what happened during those years and you'll understand what happened during the first six weeks in Texas when time vanished. Do you want me to tell you what happened? It wasn't just forty years that passed. It might have been thousands of years compressed into a split second in human three dimensional time." Ken stopped the rental car for a red light.

"You're trying to make me crazy," I said as the light turned green and we moved forward.

"Paul and I started comparing stories and figured out that the day he was trying to save you by tossing you overboard was exactly forty years before the day that you met Mary and the exact day that I threw a smoky mountain quartz crystal into Blue Lake. The theory is that those who jumped overboard, including you, suddenly went from 1943 to 1983. Perhaps you think that's just a coincidence.

111

"There's more, Daniel. On the day that I found the crystal that would eventually go to Blue Lake, Paul called me on the phone and said there was a survivor from the U.S.S. Eldridge. He was all excited that anyone had survived. It was you Daniel, you who had survived. Yet you had no way of knowing what you had survived. And it was what happened at Blue Lake that brought you home, back to three dimensions."

"I might have been an agoraphobic, but I was not traveling in time. I can account for my entire life and there are no forty year holes."

"Can't you come up with a few dinky holes?" Again the car had stopped. There was a traffic jam on the freeway. "What were you doing all those days you couldn't move from your chair, that you couldn't step out the front door of your house? Account for all those hours."

"I don't want to," I said. "Leave me alone. If it's not about the Holy Grail, I don't want to hear it."

"Listen to me. Your life in three dimensions isn't making any sense to you, is it?" Ken said, staring hard at me. I shrugged and waved my hand, signaling him to continue with his story.

"The crystal I bought in Napa that day was a beautiful smoky mountain quartz. I didn't know what it was when I bought it, but I put it in my window facing the lake.

"One night I was out on my porch. The stars were brilliant. Waves were washing up onto the beach. I could hear very clearly, the chanting. The spirits. Long ago, Clear Lake had been the hub of one of the largest Native American civilizations in California. Right across Cash Creek, where my resort was, twenty, fifty different villages had once thrived. I felt a connection with these people." Ken looked at me. "That's the fifth word. Change, Death, Time, Breath, Connection."

I didn't say a word.

"When I had decorated my resort, I did it all in Native American art. I bought beautiful statues of warriors and eagles and bears, all carved out of redwood.

"I felt very connected that night as I was looking at the stars and listening to the singing. I could hear Blue Lake, or I thought I could. That's when I got another call from Paul. I took the smoky mountain crystal I had bought in the store with me as a gift for him. He had already been in Gateways for six months and I hadn't visited him yet. Gateways was a home for the mentally disturbed.

"Paul was sitting in the garden and when I first got there, I thought he must be doing better. I told him he looked great and he didn't answer. He was just sitting there staring ahead."

"What was wrong with him?" I asked.

"Paul had remained on that vanishing ship so when time returned to normal he was still on board and it was still 1943. But there were others. You were one of the others. There were those who jumped over board. Now these men traveled forward in time. Like going from 1943 to 1983. Paul said you'd been thrown overboard and were in trouble. 'We have to help him,' that's all he kept repeating to me."

"What are you talking about? I was never in the Navy. I was never on a vanishing boat, never lost in time. Maybe in Burbank, never in time," I said sarcastically. Who is this idiot? Ken wasn't listening and he continued despite the look of incredulity on my face.

"So, I took the crystal, the smoky mountain quartz out of my pouch and handed it to Paul. He held it for the longest time saying that if he couldn't go home, the crystal should go home. And then he told me where home was.

Little did I know that I would be returning a crystal to a place white men were not allowed, had never been allowed. Paul had just been to see you at the hospital, after your surgery.

"So I returned home, thinking to myself that there was no possible way to do the favor Paul had requested. But Paul had said that if I didn't try, both you and he would die. What was I suppose to do?

"I had pictures developed of the smoky mountain quartz and wrote a letter to the Board of Governors at the Taos Pueblo in New Mexico, requesting that I be allowed to take this crystal to Blue Lake. I had to make at least one symbolic effort, for Paul's sake. Since I felt they probably got many requests, I had programmed a little double terminator quartz crystal with my intentions for Paul and you which was my only purpose at that point in time. I put the crystal in a box and sent it off in the mail. I was planning to be in Taos in about two or three weeks.

"About two weeks later I received a letter from the War Chiefs. They respected my wishes but they would not allow me to go to Blue Lake. I went to New Mexico anyway, the next week. I drove over to my uncle's house after arriving and we went to the Taos Pueblo to visit the Governor's Office. I wanted to retrieve my little crystal. It was two window crystals that were connected. I had never seen anything like it before and it was very special to me.

"I entered the Board of Governor's office and identified myself, asking to pick up my box. After leaving, I put the crystal, God's tear, in my pocket and my uncle and I went over to the cemetery. It was very old, very quaint, and there were intense feelings there, feelings of anger and hatred, rape and abuse, and I'm sure there were reasons for it all. Those feelings had been passed on from person to person and were very distorted.

"At the cemetery, I looked for Cradle Flower, who had passed long ago. It took me about an hour to find the correct headstone.

"When we found her marker, I started to pray. I felt a powerful connection to her, as if she were guiding me. I said to my uncle, 'I need her help.' Within a second he picked up a candle and said, 'She's here.'

"The candle was about a half inch in diameter and ten inches long. I lit it and held it close to my lips and felt Cradle Flower beside me, her spirit giving me strength, and I promised, 'Paul, we're not going to let you down. You're coming home, Paul. Whatever happened to you, we're getting you home.' I still have that candle today."

Ken parked the car in front of Gateways. This must be the place where Paul was living. It wasn't far from the hospital where I had my heart surgery. Gateways was a series of bungalows with flowers out front, located in a residential neighborhood. The car had stopped but neither of us got out. He continued with his story.

"I had parked our car on the other side of the Board of Governor's building next to the rest rooms. As we walked over, my uncle saw a friend coming down the road named Jimmy Remo. I knew Jimmy and my uncle had a deep respect for each other. I was introduced amidst hand shaking and warm hugs.

"We talked for awhile and then decided to go back to Jimmy's house, just down the road. When we got there, I took out the crystal I had wrapped in deerskin, the smoky mountain crystal. He looked at it and his eyes grew large. I said that I had sent a picture of this crystal to the Board of Governor's awhile back, asking if I could take this crystal to Blue Lake. He looked at me and said, 'You're the one.'

"I answered, 'Yes.'

"Jimmy said, 'This was referred to the War Chiefs and I sat in. A group of twelve decided that this would not be good. You see, we are concerned about black magic.'

"I was shocked. Later I understood. At the time I didn't realize that the Native Americans were concerned about such thing. I had so much to learn.

"We sat there in his mobile home that chilly, September day. I said, 'Did you see the little crystal that was in the box with my letter?' Jimmy said he hadn't, so I took out the crystal. It was still wrapped. Nobody had touched it. I said, 'This is for you.'

"I handed it to him and he unwrapped it, looked at it for awhile and said to me, 'I'll take you to Blue Lake.'

"I could feel a powerful connection with Jimmy. He felt like a long lost brother. Jimmy was suffering from asthma during that time and I started working with him. I was using my healing abilities on a regular basis now. As we left, Jimmy told me he would call in a week or two. It was now the second week in September.

"I was very excited that my vision for Paul was going to come true. Three weeks from my original visit, I got a phone call and Jimmy says, 'Can you come this next weekend? We're all set.'

"I arrived in Albuquerque on Friday, rented a car, and drove up. I got there about seven thirty at night. It was very cold and had been raining. I chatted with Jimmy's wife and daughter for awhile and then Jimmy and I sat down to talk. He told me he had gone to his uncle, Perona. Perona was a Kiva Indian, about seventy-six years old. He was in charge of giving spiritual instruction to the children and could teach for weeks about only the moon and the sun.

"Perona was one of the most balanced, centered, and loving beings I had ever met. Can you imagine someone teaching about the sun and the moon for one month and never picking up a book? Imagine the experience of feeling and hearing those stories as a child.

"Jimmy told me he had gone to his uncle and told him that he was going to take the crystal to Blue Lake. He asked his uncle what he thought. Perona told Jimmy that he would have to pray on it and he did. Two nights before my arrival, Perona was getting ready for bed. He took out two eagle feathers, and as he lay in bed, he crossed the feathers over his heart. Now he would meditate on the crystal, seeing in his dreams what the crystal meant.

"As he meditated with the eagle feathers crossing his heart, he had a vision. The crystal was going to change everything on earth. The crystal was going to raise the earth vibration from the heart chakra to the throat chakra." Ken looked at me and for an instant it was hard to see his face. His eyes and forehead kept fading in and out but I could hear his words.

"Jimmy, Perona and I were heading for Blue Lake the next morning at five o'clock. Blue Lake was located about forty miles northeast of the pueblo. It was very mountainous and because the first snow had already fallen, we were going to go up the river route. The mountain route was much faster but there was no way for us to cross it. We talked about the horses and at the time I didn't realize that there was going to be a problem. They were kept at pasture in a field that Jimmy had and would have to be caught the next morning.

"As I prepared for bed that evening, I could hear the wind howling outside the trailer. It was very cold and I was glad to wrap myself up in my down sleeping bag. I had brought good cold weather equipment for myself, a down jacket, powder snow suit, boots and a hat. I had also brought two rain proof ponchos.

"The next morning we got up at five o'clock and headed out as planned. We drove for awhile up to Jimmy's ranch where the horses were. When we got there, we parked the car in a little three sided shed next to a creek and Jimmy walked off to get the horses.

"He came back with only two. He said that two were all he could catch and that I would have to ride with Perona. I was very unhappy with that because the journey was forty miles each way on very rough terrain. I didn't even realize then what rough terrain meant and I'd only been on a horse three or four times. I felt close to horses but this was really the first long ride I'd ever been on.

"Perona and I had a good sized, strong horse to ride. He got on first and then I mounted up behind him, onto the blanket behind the saddle. It was snowing lightly now, but it had snowed heavily the night before.

"We started off at about six o'clock in the morning and a large owl flew over us. I knew this was a good omen.

"The journey up the river was very hard. We traversed back and forth, breaking trail as we went. There were many fallen trees, and we had to pick our path carefully through them. We brushed up against snow-laden branches and soon our clothing was covered with snow. It started to snow hard.

"I had bought a hat for the trip, an Indiana Jones sort of hat. It worked pretty well but then melted snow started to collect in the brim and form into icicles. Jimmy and Perona were only wearing plaid cotton coats so I gave them both my ponchos, not realizing that my down jacket wasn't waterproof. I was still warm and comfortable at this stage but my arms were starting to hurt from hanging onto the back of the saddle as we climbed five or six feet up and down the river bank, finding our way through the fallen trees.

"As we continued, the trail got rougher and steeper. The horses were having a very difficult time. The creek we were following would vary between twenty and thirty feet across. It was no more than one to two feet deep, and the water was flowing gently. It continued to snow.

"After we'd gone twenty miles or so, we had to climb an embankment next to the creek. We'd just crossed over a fallen tree that was partially submerged. The incline ahead of us was covered with six inches of snow. Jimmy went on ahead and his horse slipped a few times. As Perona and I started up the incline the horse jumped back a little and lost his footing. I rolled off his back and slid head first down the slope, twenty feet or so until I came to a stop next to a stump, after rolling over the fallen tree we had just crossed. I had landed on the side of the trail and the embankment dropped off in front of me another thirty feet down to the creek. It was densely covered with rocks and trees. I stood and looked up to see if Perona was okay.

"The horse kept losing his footing and, rearing forward, slipped and went over backward. As the horse fell, the tree broke loose and starting sliding down the hill after the horse. Perona was thrown clear and hit the ground hard. He rolled over and over and fell face first, into the creek. He came up quickly onto his hands and knees but only after being totally submerged for what seemed like an eternity. The horse continued sliding down the embankment until he, too, landed on his side in the creek. He stood up quickly also. The fallen tree slid down the hill directly towards me and pinned my ankle up against a stump with my upper body over the side of the embankment. Pain shot up my leg and my ankle was bent in such a way that I feared it was broken. I grabbed a couple of branches and pulled myself up, trying also to ease the pressure on my ankle.

"I hung like that, caught my breath, and looked around. It was snowing very heavily and I was soaking wet. At this point, Jimmy rode back and saw me. I yelled to him that I was okay but the fall had so forcefully knocked the wind out of Perona that he was still kneeling in the creek, trying to catch his breath. The horse was up and stood shaking in the water. He looked terrified.

"Jimmy came over to help me and couldn't get the tree off my ankle. We didn't have any ropes or tools with us at all that might have been of help, only a pocket knife. He left me for a moment to help his uncle out of the water and settled onto a rock and then he went down and got the horse and moved him over to the side.

"The tree branches hung all the way down the embankment and into the water. The root system was behind my leg. Jimmy squatted down in the water to get underneath a branch so that he could roll the tree. Now Jimmy was about two hundred pounds and very strong. He put his whole body into his efforts and the tree slowly began to roll. I pulled my foot free and knew right away that my ankle wasn't broken.

"I felt relief over my ankle but upset and angry at the same time. I didn't want anything to stop me. I didn't know how far Blue Lake was, but I knew I needed to continue even if I had to continue alone, on foot. I had to get the crystal to Blue Lake.

"By the time we helped Perona up the hill, everyone was completely soaked. It was about two o'clock in the afternoon and we were in a very bad snow storm with winds blowing the snow everywhere. Then Perona told us he had broken a couple of ribs. I was concerned that he might not be able to make it back home if I didn't help him, and hold him onto the horse. At that point, I knew we would have to turn back.

"We got Perona on the horse and I walked beside him, a hand on his leg, supporting him. By now the horse was exhausted and couldn't carry both of us. We started walking back.

"We walked for about an hour and a half until we got down into lower country and came upon a small meadow. The snow was six to nine inches deep and we decided to build a bonfire. Jimmy and I gathered moss from underneath the trees. After the fire was going, we all stood beside it and started taking off the layers of wet clothing and putting them on sticks to dry. In my backpack I had brought some French bread from San Francisco. I also had some cheese. It was the only food we had.

"After our clothes were dry and we had eaten, we headed back down the hill again, following the river. Finally we got to the road and Perona wanted to walk so I got on to ride. As I mounted, I realized how stiff and sore I actually was. My legs ached as I stretched them around the generous belly of our horse.

"When we finally made it back to Jimmy's ranch, about nine o'clock, we unsaddled the horses and turned them loose. We drove to Jimmy's house and I said good-bye. My plane was leaving the next day and, with the storm, if I didn't get out before the storm hit down lower, I might not be able to travel.

"I took off towards Albuquerque. It snowed all the way but the snow hadn't been sticking. I got in late, about one o'clock. I found a hotel and ended up using my sleeping bag since the room I got had very little heat.

"The storm howled all night long and by the next morning there was about a foot of snow on the ground. When I talked to Jimmy later, he told me it was one of the worst storms ever to hit that area. Two weather fronts had come in and hit right over the area we were riding through. In fact, so much snow fell during that winter that we wouldn't be able to get back up to Blue Lake until the following June or July.

"The next morning I caught a plane home. I had planned to see Paul but I kept putting it off because I didn't want to tell him I had failed. No, I would see him only once I had gotten the crystal back home.

"During the long wait for the snow to melt at Blue Lake, I noticed changes in the crystal. It gradually became warmer and warmer to the touch. It started pulsating. You could feel it in the house. It got so hot, the vibration of it so intense, that I could no longer touch it or be around it. Finally I took the crystal out to the back yard and I buried it, tip first, about two feet into the ground. I figured that would be the best place for it until we were ready to go back to Blue Lake. Then I called Gateway to make sure Paul was still okay and he was. I told the nurse not to tell him I had called.

"So time passed and I continued as National Sales Manager for a printing company and I also saw clients regularly. I could help them, but I didn't feel I could help my best friend. I didn't have the nerve to help someone who was so close to me. Meanwhile I read everything I could get my hands on about the Philadelphia Experiment to try to understand what Paul had been through.

"The time finally came close to when we could go back to Blue Lake. There's a big ceremony that happens every August where the whole tribe goes up to the lake. Jimmy thought that maybe the best time to go would be right after the ceremony, the third or fourth week in August. I dug up the crystal and got prepared.

"I arrived in Taos late in the afternoon and drove up to Jimmy's. I didn't have time to buy food for our trip and hoped Jimmy had taken care of our supplies and gotten something simple. Sometimes meals at Jimmy's were not quite settling for my stomach so I usually came prepared with bread and cheese. This time I would have to trust.

"When I got to Jimmy's, his friend Fred was there, and he had two Shamans with him. The Shamans were from Mexico and they came to Fred and told him that they had to prepare for a crystal that was being taken to Blue Lake. They had gone up and made a medicine wheel on the side of the hill above the pueblo. Jimmy told me about the sounds, about the singing of the crystals, about the colors and the lights during their ceremony. I'll never forget the way the Shamans looked with their leather clothes and their beads. They looked like people from two or three hundred years in the past.

"As we all sat around laughing and talking and telling stories, I took out the crystal and set it on the table. There was silence in the room.

"I talked about my vision and told them how important it was and the shamans understood. We sat silent for awhile and then Fred and his two friends left and I spent the night there with Jimmy since we were going to leave the next morning.

"Perona wasn't going with us this time. He was getting older and these trips were too hard for him. Jimmy and I would each have a horse and I knew it would be easier.

"The next morning was beautiful and sunny and cool. I could see that Jimmy had been cooking all night and preparing what I guessed was cow tongue. It was this giant, meaty hunk and I thought, 'Oh gosh, what am I going to do? I can't eat that.' He also prepared some other things, and I didn't know what they were either.

"Perona had also sent something for us and when it got close to our time to leave Jimmy took out these corn husks and in the corn husks were at least twenty to thirty different bird feathers that had been blessed and used in prayer. They were beautiful.

"We decided to tie the feathers onto the crystal. We took leather straps and tied all the different feathers and all these corn husks around the outside of the crystal and blessed it again. We wrapped it in a piece of leather and put it in our pack along with the food and set out up to Jimmy's ranch to gather the horses.

"This time we were going to take the high trail. It was much easier than following the river. Jimmy had been up a few days before and knew the trail conditions. We set off about six in the morning. It felt wonderful to be finally finishing this project. Completion.

"We finally came to the timber line and from there on only rocks and boulders lined our path. We continued climbing. We had to cross a pass which was a little over fourteen thousand feet. As we crossed over, we looked up and saw snow on the tops of the rocks at the peak and then we looked down and there was Blue Lake.

"The trail down to the lake was very steep. So steep in fact that we had to get off our horses and lead them down. When we reached the lake we looked for a place for the crystal. We found a clearing and there was a rock that jutted out into the water that we could stand on. The exposed part of the rock was about five feet square.

"Cradle Flower had given me some sacred corn meal and told me how to use it, how to do the blessing in the four directions. So I had the little pouch of cornmeal with me and also several fetishes.

"We put the crystal down, still covered in feathers. I surrounded it with fetishes and Jimmy started to sing. I took out the sacred corn meal and made the blessing north, east, south and west. It was very quiet. The lake was like glass.

"When we finished we walked over to the rock. Jimmy was going to throw the crystal and just as I set my hand on his shoulder a sound came from the lake like a tone, a note. As the tone filled the air the water started to lap the rock in little waves.

"Jimmy took the crystal in his right hand and as I stood beside him with my hand on his shoulder, he threw it. As it flew, I swear, there was immediately a change in the vibration and it went from the heart chakra to the throat chakra. Jimmy has asthma and has had asthma for a long time. As soon as that vibration, that frequency changed, it hit Jimmy so hard that he dropped to the ground, coughing and choking to get his breath.

"I got down on my knees and put my hands out in front of me, making the mudra with my thumb and forefinger. I wanted to raise the vibration again, from the throat chakra to the third eye. I concentrated and made the same sound again, this time raising the tone. At that moment, the sharpest, most painful shock hit my eyes. It was just like a knife pierce. Then I saw a symbol, a Maltese cross.

"It took about thirty minutes before both of us felt alive and okay again. Afterward, we went over to this old campsite that Jimmy had been at a few days previously. There were food bags hanging from several of the trees where supplies had been placed for safe keeping, for others coming to the lake.

"We went over to a sack that Jimmy had left on his last trip. He got it down and pulled out an aluminum foil packet of cheese. Then he took fresh bread out of his day pack. There I was eating bread and cheese, just what I wanted. I figured that if I can manifest this, thirty miles from nowhere, I can do anything. And I knew everything was going to be okay.

"We ate with relish and planned our trip home. We were going to go back out through the river route. At the beginning of the trail, the terrain was very dense. The forest had never been cleared and there hadn't been any fires in the last years to help clear away the dead growth. We had to crisscross the trail, looking for spots where the horses could travel. It took several hours to get out of that terrain and to a place where we could easily follow the trail.

"I found the place where we had fallen the previous Fall and looked down. This time it looked different. I saw the lush grass, the rocks, the heavy branched trees, all free of the snow and cold wind of the storm. As I gazed at the river and the tree tangled bank that I had slid down last Fall, linear time vanished. I saw myself as a young boy taking a crystal up to Blue Lake and it was either an initiation or something that I had to do for the tribe. I was dressed in white leather. When I got to this same place on the trail where my horse fell in this lifetime, a bear had jumped out and scared my horse. My terrified pony reared up and I fell, hitting my head on the same place that I would have struck it this time, had my foot not caught and stopped my fall, inches from the rock. I saw the whole story of how I had died and I remembered how important it was for me and my tribe to take this crystal to the lake.

"It took Jimmy and I several hours to get down to the low road. As we rode along I suddenly started seeing Beings standing on each side of the trail every ten or fifteen feet. They were dressed in their beautiful ceremonial outfits. There were no children. Most of them were old men and old women seventy, eighty years old. I would see them out of the corner of my eye. They were almost tangible, as if with more thought, they would become physical. They continued lining the trail like that for about a mile like. All different. All smiling."

"Don't tell me," I said opening the door of the car and starting to get out. "Ghosts. You're seeing ghosts. I don't want to hear anymore."

∞ 14 ∞

I got out of the car. The flowers in front of the little bungalows were blowing in a cool breeze. It didn't look like any mental hospital I had ever seen. I saw a heavy, older lady, dressed in a white nurse's uniform, carrying some towels from the rear bungalow. Ken got out of the car and asked if I would be able to walk twenty feet without the aid of a wheelchair. I said that I thought I could. "Where are we going?"

"I want you to meet him." He stopped. I stopped. "When you were thrown off the ship there wasn't enough time for you to drown. There was only enough time for civilizations to come and go and maybe thousands of years to pass, all compressed into a split second. But your rational mind isn't able to cope with thousands of years. Your conscious mind can't explain any of this to itself and therefore you call yourself mad. You find yourself in a shack in Point Reyes and Mary is asking for some water for her dog. You tell yourself, 'I must have been drunk or dreaming or sick with heart failure and in dire need of a doctor.' Or you tell yourself, 'I've been in this shack too long by myself with no one to talk to,' and you go back in your memory for the first rational, sane event you can make sense out of, and that was lying on the bed as a child, watching your uncle get dressed to go off to World War II. But you tell yourself it's 1983, not 1943. Enter Mary. Enter a mother figure, a person who might be able to understand your fears and make it all okay."

Ken stopped the lady with the towels and told her, "Paul's checking out. He'll be in my care. Tell the management that they can call my attorney if they have any questions." And with that he put a business card atop her arm load of towels. We walked to the rear bungalow where flowers were in bloom. I was saying something to the effect that I didn't think biblical heroes carried business cards when Ken knocked softly on the door.

"Paul," he called out, "are you in there? It's Ken." Then he pushed open the white and red door.

Inside it was dark and humid as if no window had ever been opened. It smelled like someone inside was taking too long to die. I could make out only a bed with a crucifix hanging above it. Above the crucifix was a hologram of what looked to me like the face of Christ. I noticed it because it shimmered and changed colors in the shaft of light that the opened door had let in. For an instant it was as if Christ was beckoning us with his outstretched hand, bidding us to enter.

I was trying to make out if there was a person inside. If there was a person inside, he wasn't lying on the bed. Then I saw him crouching on the floor in a corner of the dark room.

"Paul, is that you?" Ken called gently. The figure didn't move. Ken reached to turn on a light.

An old man was crouching in the corner, hiding his face from the light. He was sobbing, pleading like a child for Ken to forgive him. I felt like I was back in the little shack in Point Reyes minutes before Mary knocked on the door, and the last thing I wanted to do was answer the door. I was four years of age and I was fifty years of age all at the same time. I needed her yet I was afraid of her. 'Whoever you are,' I thought, 'tell me that you love me. Tell me that you forgive me.'

Ken pulled up a chair for himself and another for me, two wooden kitchen chairs, the only chairs in the room.

I couldn't see his face since Paul had it covered with his hands, but his hair was gray, the hair of a man over seventy years of age. He was no one I had ever met before, certainly not the vision that appeared to me after surgery.

"You're getting out of here," Ken told him gently. "I'm taking you to my place, Paul. Did you hear me? You're coming to live with the three of us in Texas. Daniel here needs your help on a book."

"You are Him," Paul whimpered. "I was weak. Don't you understand?"

I kept looking at that hologram of Christ, not able to stop looking at it. For the rest of the afternoon, Paul was to say nothing and Ken was to conduct a three hour long monologue about every subject conceivable to man. It was as if he feared that if he stopped talking, Paul would die right in front of him. He spoke of his childhood and all the experiences they had together. He told all of his stories again, even the story of Blue Lake, this time telling it in much greater detail. Every now and then Paul would blurt out that the hologram was Ken.

"The actual hologram project of the Sacred Heart of Christ," Ken began, directing his attention more towards me than Paul, as if he wanted to correct any misnomer that he was thinking of himself in any way as Christ, "was a project I did to generate capital to save my companies. Remember Paul, I had four resorts then and so much had been damaged by the floods. Anyway, I started a hologram company and when I did the first hologram, I believed that God worked like this: He gave me a message. 'Do a hologram of Christ. When people look at it, they will use both sides of their brain and will remember who they are'." He returned his attention to Paul. "I went to some

130

businessmen I knew and raised capital for research and development. Next, I had to find an artist who could create a figure of Christ that was only three by three inches. Well, there aren't many sculptors who do miniature portraits of Christ." He laughed, but Paul was rolled into a ball, his knees up by his chin.

"I went to New Mexico and found an artist in Santa Fe. He was very spiritual, and I commissioned him to do the image of Christ," Ken was saying, as the figure of Christ beckoned again to me. "When I got the finished bronze, it didn't look like how I perceived Christ, but nevertheless this was God doing His thing through this artist and this must be right."

Paul lowered his hands from his face and stood up. "Please leave me alone," he whimpered, in a small voice.

"Do you want to get out of here, Paul?" Ken asked, and squatted next to Paul. "I think we have given the doctors enough time, don't you. I think this is a problem doctors know little about.

"Paul, do you remember how excited I was when I received the first finished imprint plate for the hologram. I ran outside to see it in the light. There weren't any eyes, just dark pits where the eyes were supposed to be. It had looked okay in the bronze statue, so the problem never occurred to me."

"No eyes at all, just pits, just pits," Paul intoned. "Just like me. I couldn't look at you."

"There's nothing to be sorry for, Paul," Ken said reassuringly, "nothing at all. You were destined to learn about betrayal and ..."

"And you," Paul interrupted, "what were you supposed to learn?"

Ken continued, "I was desperate back then. I went to an hypnotherapist friend. He put me in an altered state, and I ask, 'Why? Why pits?' And a voice said, just like this, 'Because they can't see Me'." Ken paused for a long moment and then looked at me. "Paul, the image was dead, lifeless. I knew it wasn't right and I had to tell the Board of Directors that I had made a mistake."

"So, I searched for another sculptor. I found a woman who did small carvings in clay with dental tools. I was to meet with her on Saturday. On the Wednesday before, I got home very late, around eleven o'clock, and the stars were out. I parked my car, gathered up my things, got out and turned to close the car door. Then, directly above me, these two angels flew over. I'd never seen angels before, never seen anything like this. They were almost transparent, just silhouettes without a lot of detail and their bodies tapered into cloud wisps. They flew over very slowly. I thought it was a fantastic sight, but I didn't know what it meant."

Paul bowed his head to the floor and quietly said, "I am paying homage to the dead, to all those who betray what they love most."

Ken put his arms about Paul and told him, "Paul, you remember. I got to the artist's house on Saturday and when she opened her door there were my two angels again, painted in a picture on the wall behind her. I thought, 'Yes. This is my sign. We're going to get this project completed just as God intended. He has given me this unmistakable sign and now it's His turn to work through this artist."

Paul had not moved. His forehead was still touching the floor.

"The artist completes the sculpture and I did the holography again. Now, the image still didn't look right to me but I thought, 'Well, this has to be right. This is what God has inspired her to do.' When I showed the image to other people, nobody knew who it was. Now I'm thousands of dollars into this project and I still don't have anything marketable to show to the Board.

"I then have a realization. I finally understand that this is my dream and my responsibility and the image is supposed to look like my interpretation of Christ. I also knew that by doing this so many times, I was becoming very good at holography. For the next hologram I planned to do five holograms in one by combining several fields and creating a hologram within a hologram. I planned on staying with the artist the last two weeks, working hand in hand until my vision was realized. As a result of this whole project, I had finally figured out that when I had a dream, it was my dream, and the divine direction would come to me. Right, Paul?

"During this whole holography period, I was also having vivid dreams about a space ship from Sirius. That same ship appeared in my hologram after it was produced. To me it felt as though this ship was the only thing that could survive the apocalypse and make it to the new world of the heavens."

∞ **15** ∞

A new and awesome stillness had descended upon our little group as all three of us returned to Texas. We had been gone less than twenty four hours. When we returned to the house on the eighth hole of the Wood Creek Golf Course, Mary was not there. Evidently, she had taken off to see her horse, stabled in San Antonio. She had left only a note behind, sealed in a legal size envelope, by way of explanation. The dog was with the neighbors, happy as a lark.

All the telephone could do was ring over and over again without anyone answering it. Ken was too busy helping Paul, the hologram still pressed to his forehead, into a tiny guest bedroom sandwiched between the washer and dryer on one side and a door to the garage on the other. He was tall and bony, almost gangling in the way he moved. His gray hair hung down almost to his waist giving him a wild look, his bumpy large nose and thick chapped lips preparing you for the huge deep set greenish eyes that changed color depending on the light. He had huge hands and feet, not the hands and feet of a thin man but of a large boned primitive man, who I imagined would have been at home with the land and planting seeds in the earth. His teeth were yellowish and his mouth opened too wide for the words he was saying. As he pressed the hologram to his forehead, it was the pose of a man both hurt and praying to some unknown gods. He didn't lie on the guest room's bed, but sat cross legged on the floor, his forehead touching the floor as though he was perpetually bowing. All he would have required was a chant and you might well have taken him for a badly dressed shaman. His shirt and trousers were bleached blue jeans and he had, even on the plane, refused to wear shoes.

I went next door to retrieve Polarity for company and waited. An hour later, Ken came to my bedroom and said, "I guess we'll have to cook for ourselves tonight." I followed him out into the kitchen and watched as he opened the refrigerator.

He placed a couple hot dogs in the microwave on a plate and pushed the start button. We both watched the cooking hot dogs. "I'll take care of Paul," he said.

The microwave's beep sounded, he opened the door, and reached for the plate. It was too hot and he sucked on his burnt fingers. "Mary can take it out of there with her bare hands," he laughed, "I wonder how she does it."

"Gets her hands from her grandmother on her mother's side," I said. "There was an amazing woman."

He took a bite, but again it was too hot and he had to wait. "You want anything to eat?"

I hadn't eaten for the last twenty four hours, but I wasn't hungry. "No thanks."

He took another swipe at the hot dog with his teeth, deciding this time to endure the pain. "Maybe time is too much for us," Ken said drying his hands.

"Look," I said, "assuming we're both crazy and I see no decent reason why we shouldn't assume that, let's pretend that all time is eternally present. Do you know what happens if what T. S. Eliot said is really true? It means we ate of the fruit of the tree of the understanding of good and evil and we are like God, just like the devil promised we would be."

∞ 16 ∞

It was dawn, a different dawn. I didn't know what I was understanding, but I was to understand something. I opened my sliding glass door and called Polarity to come inside the house. Dog skids across wooden deck, rushing to my door. No sooner was he in than he wanted to get out again, and then back in. I opened the glass door and sat back down in my rocker. I closed my eyes. The dog took this as a cue to leap up into my lap. Dog kisses.

All through the night, I had heard no sound that Ken was even alive. Several times I had checked to see if his bedroom door was open. It was tightly shut. I checked to see if Paul was awake. His door, also, was tightly shut, no thread of light appearing from underneath. Once I thought I heard Ken on the telephone and wondered if he was talking to Mary then decided that whether he was or wasn't, was none of my business. As for Polarity, he seemed oblivious to his master's departure except for the fact that he was all over me with a new flurry of doggy devotion and neediness.

Outside my sliding glass door, the sky was dark over cast and I wanted something to think about other than what I was thinking about. The creek's black surface was unbroken by the glint of night crystals. I lit a cigarette and stared at the water, hoping to catch the random movement of a turtle or fish.

"Polarity, outside before it rains," and I got out of my chair, opening the sliding glass door and letting the dog out onto the covered deck. The dog tore down to the opposite end of the deck where the master bedroom was and then back up to my end of the deck with a red rubber ball in his mouth, screeching to a stop, paws up on my sliding glass door, red ball still in his mouth. He lost his grip on it and re-caught it between his teeth.

"Stay outside," I commanded.

Polarity bounded up and down, red ball in mouth, paws scratching on the glass. Since Mary wasn't here, once again Polarity was my dog. He attacked the basketball, with a vengeance, red ball still in his mouth, playing with both balls at the same time.

I opened the sliding glass door and went out on the deck to sit in a wooden rocking chair and smoke and throw the wet, red rubber ball the dog was pushing into my lap, then grabbing back then shoving hard against my chest, as if to remind me that I wasn't doing my duty. I lit the cigarette, watching the rippling waters of the creek, the island floating in the center, and the twiggy trees and rocks reflected deep in the green, green waters. I would look at scenery when I needed a message from the gods, believing for a split instant that an omen would be available for my brilliant interpretation. The winds were starting up, rippling the waters, bending the grasses, blowing through the trees. Was it possible that what we thought of as madness was but other dimensions of time, other lives, all of them extremely present, all of them creating what we call the present, this very instant in time? Was it possible that any human who'd seen Jesus suffer and die would ever be the same again? Would anyone ever be able to separate their horror from their salvation? When I thought of it, it felt as if my face was turning black, due to the immensity of the sorrow and suffering. All time, all history is now. Human kind doesn't require any more enlightenment, only the courage to face what they already feel and can't help but feel, over and over and over again and again. Polarity, tell me, is that the secret of the Holy Grail? Let go of your life in order to expand your life, even unto the ends of the earth?

I threw the ball to the other end of the deck, the dog taking off, slipping and sliding before he could finally get a grip and actually move forward. Then back he would prance, ball proudly between his teeth.

I thought of going into the kitchen to make a cup of coffee, which hopefully would improve the taste of my cigarettes. Today, they tasted like glue and hot burning grass. "Polarity, inside," I ordered, getting to my feet and ushering him back into my bedroom and through the hallway. The dog bounded joyfully on his way to the kitchen, knocking his water dish against the wall and spilling waves all over the floor.

The door to the master bedroom was still shut. If Ken wasn't as yet awake, my grinding the coffee was sure to awaken him. Get coffee beans from freezer, get filtered water, grind coffee beans from freezer, pour water into pot, insert paper filter into brown plastic filter holder, put coffee beans back in freezer, the airplane like roar of the grinder. Console the dog who can't find his ball and is scurrying about, madly searching.

The coffee drips. I open the front door. Outside is a brand new day, with big thunderclouds looming Texas style. Out front the puppy can get a good grip on the grass and accelerate quick in search of lost balls, which are in the back on the deck, and not in front. Through the trees he rockets, circling the yard, circling the cars, having abandoned balls in favor of going for a ride, or so he thinks.

Across the tree-lined lane, is the eighth hole of the Wood Creek golf course. No golfer is about at this early

138

hour of morning. Dew on the grass glitters in a thin shaft of sun light, creating crystal nets for God's invisible fishermen. My second cigarette tastes worse than the first, and I snub it out before it's half completed. One needs coffee before one can smoke.

Polarity ran in ever widening circles, searching, barking out his excitement at what he wasn't finding. Then he'd come trotting towards me panting, tongue hanging out of the side of the mouth, hair a frazzle, and sit obediently, the good dog at my feet pleading with me to help. Human beings are good for something. We not only can throw the ball, we can find the ball that dogs have lost. We are dog Gods.

Ken was standing in the doorway drinking a cup of MY coffee. I had eaten enough of HIS food, so he could partake of MY coffee. He had his long silvery hair pulled back into a pony tail. His glasses glinted in the ever growing shaft of sun. He was watching the dog, then the sky, stretching far out in front of him.

"Coffee's ready," he called.

"Storm's coming," I called.

"I'll get you a cup. Black, right?" He turned and went back inside the house. Polarity, thinking he was missing something, tore after him and screeched to a stop at the open door, deciding that it wasn't wise to get trapped inside the house. Then, re-changing his mind, he sets a cautious foot inside and then dashes in and I hear him slipping and slithering his way about the kitchen. I hear Ken's 'good morning' and 'now, take it easy' directed dogward.

Ken appears again at the door, almost tripping over Polarity, both of them trying to get out of the house at the same instant in time. He winces. Polarity charges, making yet another circle of the cars, hoping Ken would be the one to take him for a ride. Ken handed me my coffee, trying not to trip over the dog as Polarity flew past on his second circling of the fortress. I spill the hot coffee over my thumb and forefinger, sip at it and try to think of something to say. Two men drinking coffee in the early morning golf course sun. Healthy male bonding.

"By the way, I checked on Paul at three," I said. "Do you think he's any better?"

Silence. Sip coffee. Once again I remind Polarity that all the balls are in the back, on the deck, and not in front where the cars could run over them.

"I called my mother," he said. "She'll come and help take care of Paul if we need her." The 20th century version of Joseph of Arimathæa seemed content with that alternative, and finished his coffee, going back into the kitchen for a refill. This time he didn't come back out and both I and Polarity tore into the kitchen after him before he had closed the door to the bedroom.

"Do you really . . . No, forget it. I guess it no longer matters," I said, entering the kitchen and tripping over Polarity. But then I couldn't stop myself and blurted out, "It's bullshit, Ken. Paul is sick." Suddenly I felt like a fool. If he was sick, what was I? Who was I to accuse anyone of being mentally deranged. I forged ahead anyway, beginning to lose my temper.

"What Paul and I need is a life, not some childish ideas about time and magical boats that whiz back to the time of Christ."

"The doctors did their best. Now it's my turn."

"To do what?"

"You'll see. Be sure you're home tonight. Wherever Paul and I journey, I want you to come along." There was a long pause. "Daniel, all you have to do is remember."

∞ **17** ∞

The storm had been building all day. All the sun lit crystals in the creek had vanished. Thunder rattled the window panes of the house just like Texas thunder storms are suppose to.

From my rocking chair I could see and hear everything, even the squawking of the ducks on the creek. I stared at the darkening sky and then at the telephone, wishing someone, anyone, would call me.

The puppy was no doubt under Ken's bed for he didn't much care for Texas thunder storms. I closed my eyes. Suddenly, I saw my father's face again but I couldn't keep looking at it, or at the sky, which had become even darker, as if night had decided to fall too quickly, or the dirt and the blood and the smell had obscured the sun, never to let it be seen again.

In my mind's eye my father was telling me to breathe through my mouth and that everything depended upon it, for we could not betray Him, not now. I saw the tree posts standing upright, covered in dirt, waiting. They were no higher than six feet, which was why it was difficult to see them, only the height of a man, no higher. Three skinny men standing in front of the rest of the crowd, three unfinished scarecrows without arms or heads.

Just then the phone rang and I was awakened from my slumber. It was Jon, my friend from Berkeley, calling to see how I was. He was the last person I wanted to talk to now.

"Jon," I said recalling my slumbering day dream, "You don't really want to know how I am, do you?"

"So, have you figured out if you're losing your mind?"

"Yeah," I said.

"Yeah what?" he asked.

"Jon, it's real ding batty here in Texas. Don't move here, whatever you do."

"Don't like cowboy hats. So tell me, what's going on?"

"You ever heard of a ship vanishing into thin air?"

"You're certainly big on the invisibility factor, aren't you?"

"What does that mean? What if I'm clinically mad?" I said, not giving him a chance to answer.

"I think we should arrange a code word. You say 'Unified Field Theory' and I'll organize a rescue team to come down there and save your ass from the lunatic fringe. Are you sane enough to remember anything about 'Unified Field Theory'?"

"I know it was Einstein. He's guru of the nuts nowadays."

"But Albert doesn't explain your memory lapses. You were a different person after your heart surgery, but who wouldn't be if they had a heart that wasn't working correctly."

"What do you mean, I was a different person?"

"I don't know. It's hard to describe. Daniel, don't start thinking in those paranoid terms or you'll drive yourself into believing what Ken believes. Don't you dare become invisible on me."

I didn't have the chance to continue because I heard shouting from the kitchen area, accompanied by rolling thunder.

"Look, Jon, I think all hell is breaking loose in the kitchen," I said. "I'll call you later if I'm still alive."

I hung up the phone and made my way out of the bedroom through the little hallway and into the kitchen where Paul was standing with a pocket knife, waving it in front of Ken's face. Ken was standing quietly, and appeared to be trying to reason with his friend.

"You are Him," Paul shouted. "You are the one I betrayed."

"Calm down, Paul," Ken was saying.

"Tell me it's not Your picture," Paul pleaded. "Tell me. I dare You."

Tears were streaming down Paul's face and his voice was high pitched, almost a squeak of pain. All I could think of to do was go into my bedroom and call the local SWAT team. Paul was drawing closer to Ken with the knife and Ken was wisely backing away. It was obvious he couldn't see Ken but knew where he was from the sound of his voice.

"Who?" Ken asked. "Who do you think I am, Paul? Tell me."

"Christ, the one I killed ...," Paul shrieked, and thunder sounded like ten metal garbage cans rolling down a long flight of stairs. I thought I could hear Polarity yelping on the deck.

"See, I know who You are. I know who You are," Paul cried in anguish. "It was Your eyes floating in mid air. Your eyes looking at me with love even though I'd betrayed You."

Ken had stopped backing up and was standing still, letting Paul come ever closer, brandishing the knife, his face lit up now and then by the lightning. "Oh Lord, I tried, I tried to defend You, remember? Remember the garden, when the soldiers came?" Paul raised his knife in the air. "Do You see them? They are coming. Be still. I will defend Thee! I am he. I am Peter who cut off the Roman's

143

ear!" Paul swung the knife violently, attacking someone only he could see. The blade caught Ken in the thigh, ripping the trousers. Blood immediately gushed forth, soaking into Ken's trouser leg. Paul opened his eyes wide, his body frozen. "Do you hear it?" he asked.

Ken grabbed his leg, a grimace of pain crossing his face as he said calmly, "Paul. Paul, it's me, Ken. Hold on there, buddy."

"Do you hear it? Listen," Paul whispered.

"What?" Ken asked, "What do I hear?"

"The rooster. Cock-a-doodle do," Paul said and cupped a hand to his ear and listened. "Cock-a-doodle do," he cried again, "Cock-a-doodle do." Paul was sobbing as he said, "The rooster crows thrice. I am a dead man."

Except for the sound of the rain beating on the roof, all was silent. Ken was holding his leg, in an attempt to stop the blood, but as I looked at him, I could see that it wasn't his wound he was worried about. It was, of all things, the dog that now concerned him.

"Polarity," came Ken's voice. Paul was again kissing the floor as Ken rushed from the kitchen. I hurried into the living room and opened the sliding glass door. Thirty mile an hour winds, filled with rain, blew into my face. I stumbled out onto the deck. It was afternoon and as dark as night.

"Polarity," I yelled, and then I saw Ken, wet hair in his eyes and one leg of his trousers half red with the blood.

Ken was shouting, "He got out. Where the hell's Mary, she's supposed to be home by now."

Whatever poise he had once possessed had deserted him. He was like me, stumbling in the rain and the wind, while Paul wailed from the kitchen that he had just taken the light breath.

"Ken, we have to get you to a doctor," I yelled. "The dog was frightened by the storm, I'll get him. He probably ran around to the front. I'll get him. Go and take care of your leg."

I made my way, dripping, back to the front door, hoping that Polarity would be huddled there waiting to get in. But just as I yanked the front door open, I heard the screech of tires and a thud and Paul screaming that the giant eye had returned and was going to kill him.

"Polarity," Ken shouted again.

When I reached the driveway, all I saw were two headlights and the sheets of rain.

"Eyes, my eyes, why hast thou forsaken me?" Paul was screaming from inside the house.

"He ran out in front of my car," pleaded a woman's voice. "I couldn't stop. He just ran right out in front of my car. Let me help." The woman driver ran towards me, calling over the beating of the wind and rain. Then, she too, stopped, realizing there was nothing she could do. She tried to wipe the rain from in front of her face, and at her feet lay the red ball the puppy had been looking for.

Suddenly, another set of headlights was pulling into the driveway. "I didn't see him," the woman driver cried out. "He darted out in front of the car and I couldn't stop in time. You understand, don't you?"

But I wasn't looking at her. I was watching Mary's truck pull up.

"There was no way anyone could have stopped," said the woman, as Mary hurriedly got out of her truck, arms full of groceries, a puzzled look on her face.

Ken was standing in the rain. She called to him, but he didn't turn around. Mary called out again with a questioning, "What's up?" She wasn't looking at Ken, or if she was she hadn't as yet seen his bloody trouser leg.

145

"I tried to stop," said the woman driver to Mary, the rain pouring off her bleached blond hair. "The dog shouldn't have been allowed out of the house."

Mary's body seemed to go slack and the expression on her face melted. She wasn't looking at the stranger, she was only looking at Ken's back.

"What happened?" she cried.

Ken slowly turned around. The dog's white and black coat was drenched with rain, and blood. The rain was coming down hard, as though trying to wash the dog's coat clean. Mary dropped her two brown paper sacks to the pavement, and emitted a muffled, anguished cry. She knew. She tried to reach forward and take the puppy up in her arms, as though carrying him away from the scene would help, help her.

"He's gone," Ken said, his eyes full of rain. "He was frightened, Mary. He was frightened by the storm."

The lady driver already had her arms full of the groceries and was asking what she could do with them.

Ken told me to go inside and he gently thanked the lady driver for her concern and instructed her to get home, out of the rain. I went inside and waited. I could just barely see Ken and Mary, through the glass panes in the door. They were huddled together, in the back seat of the truck, holding onto what lay in Mary's lap.

∞ 18 ∞

"You must be Daniel, the writer. I'm Nita Page, Ken's mother," a petite, attractive woman said, standing in the open doorway. Over her head, I saw a taxi cab pull away.

She gave me a quick look that stopped me from finishing the sentence I hadn't even begun. Then she peered out the window above the kitchen sink and evidently saw what she was looking for. Not taking her eyes off the sight, she asked again, though it was actually for the first time, what was happening.

"Everyone is dying," Paul shouted from the guest room, in ponderous deep tones. She looked at Paul as he made his way into the dining room.

"The dog was frightened by the storm," I tried to explain. "Ken and Mary are outside, in the truck."

Nita took a deep breath and then turned to look at Paul. "Everyone is not dying, do you hear me, Paul? Everyone is not dying." Then she went out the front door. I saw her walk to the truck and open the driver's door.

What she saw inside made her back away, hands rushing to her face. Then she approached the truck again, and stood there talking with Ken and Mary. After a while she reached into the cab and took the dog from Mary's arms and carried him to the rear of the house. I heard her call my name. She was standing in their bedroom by the sliding glass door to the deck and holding the dog in her arms. Beside her was a Nordic Track exercise machine on one side and the large, queen size bed with a soft metal gray comforter on the other. "Go into the garage and find me a shovel. I'll wait for you here."

I did as she told me. The garage was hot and humid. One bare light bulb lit up all the paraphernalia they had collected during the years. I had no idea where a shovel would be located. On a far wall hung two large rakes and a broom and I thought a shovel might be in that vicinity. Sure enough, behind a green, rubber trash container stood a brand new shovel, the paper sticker still pasted on the bright shiny metal. I freed it and took it back inside to where Nita was waiting.

She didn't even look at me but when she felt I was coming she pried open the sliding glass door with her right foot and went out onto the deck. Carrying the shovel, I followed her. That is when I saw Ken standing in the rain staring at us, but I'm not sure that he really saw us. His clothes were drenched by the downpour, but he seemed not to notice. Now and again a sliver of lightening could be seen illuminating the blackness of the sky. No one said a word. He opened the wire gate for his mother. He made a gesture to the effect that he would carry the dog's body but Nita would have none of it.

The ground was half grass, half mud as she made her way down to the river and along the bank with Ken bringing up the rear. When she reached an open patch of grass, she came to a stop. She stood there for the longest time. The clouds had parted just enough for a moon to make its brief appearance. Its light wouldn't last long for already the storm clouds were threatening to obscure what light there was. Cold, frosty crystal patches shimmered in the water. Ken began to dig, never flinching with pain from his gashed leg.

If the earth had been dry, the digging would have been harder but now, with the rain as preparation, the earth was soft and the blade slid easily underneath the grass and came up full of rich black earth covered with the thinnest blanket of green grass. Nita kept her eyes focused on every move the shovel made as though nothing was as important as the depth of the small grave.

When Ken had finished, Nita nodded her head, sank to her knees and carefully and slowly placed the dog in the earth. She stayed there not moving, not looking at anything, no one moving, no one looking at anything as the rain continued to fall. A thunder cloud had made the river dark and for an instant I couldn't see my hand in front of my face. It was an eerie kind of darkness because it had descended so completely. All I could do for that instant was to listen to the rain on the grass, the rain in the water, the rain dripping through the trees and falling to the earth.

I heard the sound of footsteps approaching and Mary's voice. I had no idea how anyone could have come down the hill in the blackness. Mary was calling out to Ken to see where he was. She was carrying the fang dented Frisbee in one hand, Polarity's favorite. She bent over and placed it in the grave beside him. It was a long time before she stood up and wiped the rain from her eyes. I heard Ken say softly, "I love you." I heard Mary's soft tears accompanied by the rain on the grass. I heard the urgent words 'husband', 'family' and 'always' and the wind was blowing my hair in my face and I didn't know whether it was Mary or Polarity that I found so hard to release. I heard the sound of the shovel digging into the pile of wet earth and the earth thudding into the hole in the ground.

After a while those sounds also stopped. The rain continued to fall blown by stiff cold winds. The thunder cracked without lightening as if it no longer had any need of lightening. The leaves of the trees struggled against the wind. My clothes were soaked, and I wondered why we were waiting.

Ken's mother was the first to start up the hill towards the house. I followed her, leaving Mary and Ken by themselves, their silence filling the blackness of the night.

Inside Nita washed her hands in the kitchen sink and then went to the guest room to see how Paul was doing. I sat alone in the kitchen, never so alone in my life. I heard Mary and Ken enter the house. Ken went into their bedroom, asking over his shoulder what clothes Mary wanted him to pack. Mary followed him into the room and I could see her sitting on the edge of the bed.

"Don't you really want me to stay here with you?"

"No. I want you safe. Please. Go see your parents. Okay? Do it for me. Look, with Paul like he is and now Polarity..." he paused. "I know how upset you are, we both are, but I have to do this with Paul now. This can't wait and I need to know you're in a safe place so I won't have to worry about you."

"Okay," Mary said, almost in a whisper.

Minutes later, Ken emerged from the bedroom with a flight bag fully packed. He called a cab, and Mary and he sat on the front porch to wait. Soon, I heard the heavy slam of a car door and then the front door open and close. I saw Ken go into the living room. I had no idea what he was doing.

Then Nita entered the kitchen and I was glad for someone to talk with, to share my despair. "Maybe I shouldn't have come here," I said.

"You know why you're here," she said looking straight at me, just like my mother would.

"What do I know?"

"One of Ken's biggest issues is one of your issues also, isn't it? In fact, it's an issue for every creature on this planet. Relationships. It's always about relationships." She continued, "Do you know why Ken relates to the issue of abandonment and relationships the way he does?"

"Should I?" I asked.

"It's because in a past life, and also in this lifetime, he was forced to leave his children. Do you know what the crystal chalice is?"

"The Holy Grail."

"We search hard trying to remember, like you are trying to remember, like we all are trying to do." Nita smiled. "Memory. It's one of the words of the Holy Grail. Do you know the others?"

"I now know six. Change. Death. Time. Breath. Connection. And Memory. And the seventh?"

Nita pretended as though she hadn't heard. She said I should go into my room and rest, that she would call me when everyone was ready. On leaving the room, she turned, and answered me, "The seventh word is the hardest one of all."

"But why memory? Why is memory the sixth word?"

"You haven't seen one of Ken's workshops, have you Danny?"

"No, I don't believe in all that stuff," I answered honestly.

"You don't believe that people can really feel and experience glimpses of who they really are and or who they were. That is exactly what you have been going through up here. That is what your visions, your so called madness has been trying to tell you."

"But how do you know people aren't just making up all these past lives which Ken seems to take so seriously."

"It doesn't matter if they are or not. You're a writer, what does the word 'imagination' mean to you?"

151

"But doesn't there have to be a difference between what is imagined and what is real, I mean what you can feel and touch and see?"

"So what is that difference, Danny? If you know what it is, tell me."

"Nita, if that difference doesn't exist, anything can be as real as that chair you are sitting on. And then the world is chaos."

"The world is nothing other than stories about stories about stories. The world is metaphors piled on top of each other staring at each other in the mirror. All you see and touch and smell and feel are just stories, Danny. We humans find it convenient to rank that 'sensory' story at the top of the list and give it special importance, but it is still just a story, it still exists only in the world of imagination when you really get down to it."

"But how can you live any life based on that kind of thinking? A person would go mad if they tried."

"And madness is nothing but another story you're telling yourself. Death is also nothing but a story. We cannot know what death is, so we imagine it. Ken has worked with over six thousand people, doctors, lawyers, heads of business, professors, therapists, people from all over the world. You should hear the stories they tell in order to explain their pain. Pain also is another story, another energy. But if you change the story, you change the reality. People are alive today who wouldn't be alive had Ken not worked with them. And all because they were willing to change, to transform their story." She looked down at her hands on the table, rubbed a lingering smear of mud and sighed. "You should go to one of his workshops and see what happens for yourself. Or just sit here and wait and you will see what I mean. He's going to work with Paul like only he can do."

"And the dog's death? Was that also just another story. A woman driver can't stop fast enough in the rain and a much loved friend is suddenly dead. What purpose did that little story accomplish?"

"Danny think about what it is you're feeling. Forget everything else. Focus on the feeling for that's what's real. Polarity is no longer a physical being but don't you dare say he does not exist. That dog is more alive now than ever. Can't you feel it. We are not crying because the dog is gone; we are crying because he is all too much with us. That puppy is perhaps more real now than anything you can touch, eat or smell. Look, when Jesus was crucified I believe that no one who was able to look at that sight would say it was just another death, that the criminal was no longer with us, that Jesus Christ was nothing but a handful of dust and blood. He was so alive on that day that He gave birth to all of Christianity and it changed the face of the earth. Danny, it wasn't because Christ was dead that Christianity was born. It was because He was alive. The earth has yet to see a life that stupendous, that miraculous and dazzling. Don't you remember, Danny? You also were there. Ken was holding you by the hand. Don't you remember?"

Standing up, she took me by the hand and literally dragged me into my bedroom where all the videos of Ken's workshops were stacked. She turned on the television and slipped one into the VCR. She then told me to sit down and watch and not move, not move a muscle.

The video tape began with a scene of people lined up and waiting to get into some conference room. A large sign beside the entrance read, "Multidimensional Cellular Healing." There were men and women and an occasional teenager, dressed in everything from shorts and blue jeans to their Sunday best. Some of the people were obviously

153

disabled. "Most of these people are in pain," Nita was saying. "They are suffering from fear, anger, cancer, heart disease, you name it. And what they believe they are suffering from is what they will tomorrow be able to teach others to conquer. What you most dread and fear is your greatest teacher."

∞ **19** ∞

Paul was lying on the living room sofa, a light sheet covering his body. A pillow sat on the floor by Paul's feet, as if that too was one of the tools of the ceremony that was about to take place. Ken had lit two bundles of sage, one near Paul's head and the other near his feet. He was wearing shorts and a clean white shirt. A bandage stained with blood was wrapped around his right thigh. Once again, Paul had the small hologram pressed to his forehead just as he had all the way from Northern California to Texas. Nita was seated in the dining area, watching the scene from a distance. She sat with remarkably straight posture and seemed to be guarding over our little group. Ken gestured to me to sit in a large chair on one side of the fireplace with a clear view of what would be taking place.

When Ken finally took his place kneeling beside Paul, he was quiet for a long while before beginning to speak.

"Maybe," he began, looking at me, "I shouldn't have suggested you come to Texas. If so, I take the blame for what has happened. I just thought it would be possible for the three of us to do something together, but the more you try to help someone, the more you can be blamed for wanting to control them. I'm sorry."

I said nothing and waited for him to continue.

"You remember being on that ship as a little boy, don't you?" Ken said to me.

I nodded affirmatively.

"What else do you remember?"

"I don't know what I remember any more."

"Not any of it? Or are your ideas about reality too much in the way?"

"How do you know if you're making it up or it's real?"

"It doesn't matter. Tell yourself you are just making it all up. That will keep the ego quieted down. What is the first image that comes to mind? Now, just go with it, no matter how crazy it seems."

I looked around. "I think Paul needs your help more than I do."

"You might try to answer my question."

"I don't want to be your patient," I said.

"Why?" Ken asked.

"Because I just can't believe what you believe," I shot back.

"Think back. It was long ago when it started."

"Look, Paul needs your help, not me."

"Tell me, why do you keep saying that?" Ken asked gently.

"What? What do I keep saying?" I felt frustrated, angry and agitated. Why was I getting all worked up?

"That Paul, and not you, requires my help."

"Isn't that what we're all here to watch you do? Work a miracle?"

"What miracle?"

"How the hell should I know? Maybe you're going to give sight to the blind."

"What would that convince you of?"

"That the whole thing was staged for my benefit." I wanted out of here in the worst way. I felt something was going to happen and it scared me.

"No matter what happens, you won't believe it, will you?" Ken turned to Paul and said, "Paul, listen to me.

I'm just going to run my hand above your head." He closed his eyes, and ran his open hand, palm down, briefly across the crown of Paul's head. Then he opened his eyes again. "Keep your eyes open right now, so you're aware of what I'm doing. See, I'll use my hand like this. I won't touch you unless I tell you first, okay?"

Again, Paul didn't move, didn't stop pressing the hologram against his forehead. For the longest time Ken waited, as if searching for some form of clarity.

"All I want is for you to feel perfectly safe. I'm going to wait until everyone in the room is safe, so we all can feel calm." And with that he stared straight ahead and we waited. Paul lay there, as if dead. "Paul, all we are going to do is look for patterns. Patterns that exist in the part of you that knows all about you, patterns that your subconscious mind is giving energy to. When I ask you a question, I want you to tell me the first thing that comes to mind. Whatever it is, it will be the correct answer. Paul, I don't want you to judge the information. Just trust." Again, he waited, and then said, "Okay. Now I'm going to pass my open hand above your head. All right?" Paul was motionless, not making a sound. Ken raised a hand to the top of Paul's head and passed his hand a couple of inches above the crown area. "Once you understand the truth of what you are learning and creating, that energy pattern can be released. We want to see the truth of all your realities, physical, emotional, mental, and spiritual. Paul, when you really know and understand something, there is nothing more powerful. Then you will no longer need other energies. When we find a pattern, we will follow it back to the time or the event where it was imprinted. All you have to do is to tell me the first, the very first thing, that comes to your mind. Do you understand?"

When again there was no answer, Ken briefly passed his hand above Paul's forehead for the third time. For an instant, it looked to me as if his hand couldn't go any further. Ken closed his eyes for a moment and then lowered his hand to directly above the place on Paul's forehead where Paul was holding the hologram. I could see Ken's hand trembling. "It's around his head and eyes, and around the throat and chest, where I feel it the most strongly. Daniel, can you feel it in your eyes and chest? Can you feel that?"

I didn't answer.

"And the heart... and then it eases up... can you feel the heart's heat?"

I could feel a fever deep in my eyes and forehead, but I assumed it was my own imagination.

"I call upon your guides and angels to be with you. I call upon my guides and angels to be here now, to hold a space, a safe place, so that everything is exactly the way you wish it to be. Listen now, Paul. Always tell me the first thing that comes to your mind." As if verifying what he had felt, Ken again scanned Paul's eyes and forehead.

"Now remember, we all imagine different ways, some of us see, some of us feel, and some of us hear. However your information comes to you, just know that it's perfect, and remember to tell me the very first thing that comes to mind, when I ask you a question. Just let the answers come, be curious and observe."

A bolt of lightening outside the sliding glass door lit up the room. Startled, I opened my eyes and then closed them again.

"Now, what I'm going to do, and I'll be very gentle, Paul, I'm just going to put my hand on your forehead." Ken put his hand over Paul's hand, the hand that pressed the hologram so tightly to his forehead, and said, "I believe there's an energy there and we want to understand it. You're safe. I'm holding the space. I'm holding the energy in place. Just separate yourself from it, be curious and observe. Now, I want to speak to the energy around you. I want to speak to that energy. If that energy could speak to me now, what would it say?"

"I hate you. I want to kill you. Blindness," Paul screamed out. "Blindness."

"What's your name?"

"Traitor," Paul said, now sounding small and exhausted. "I'm the betrayer."

"How are you affecting Paul?" Ken asked.

"I'm killing him and blinding him. I don't want him to see the truth."

"Are you the one who's making him feel and act the way he does?"

"Yes. I'm making him crazy."

"How are you affecting the planet today?"

"You are a fool," mocked the voice. "Do you hear me? You are a fool. That you would ask such a question shows that you are a fool. And I am the one who made you a fool. I am the one who blinded you. All I need to do is whisper and all hell opens up on planet earth. Hades bubbles to the surface screaming its heebee-jeebees, laughing, mocking and betraying even the God-Man himself. I am betrayal."

"You no longer can do this. Paul is changing. He is becoming invisible. You will not be able to see him any longer. I know a place where you can go and evolve and be more than you can be. Look up with your spiritual eyes and what do you see?"

Paul's body relaxed and he said, "I see a golden light."

"I call for the guides and the angels to step out of the light. And who steps out of the light to be with you?"

A blinding flash of light shot through the room and this time the glare, the brilliance remained in the air like a light bulb that couldn't be turned off. I sat there, my eyes wide open, not believing what I was seeing, sure I was hallucinating along with the rest of them. I rubbed my eyes and looked around and the light was still in the room and I wasn't the only one who was seeing it. Paul's eyes seemed to be flooded with it as though his retinas had been painted silver. It was as if the light had become a cloud and the cloud had become a face and the face had become all that was.

"It's You," Paul screamed. "It's the Messiah come to save us, to smother the wicked and lost with love."

"Now I ask Christ to hold this Energy that's been on Paul and this planet. Hold it tight. I ask Christ to send down angels, guides and healers to be with Paul and how many does Christ send?"

Paul answers, "Nine."

"These guides, angels and healers will stay with you. They will never take your energy nor interfere in your life path. They are here to bring love and balance to your physical, emotional, mental and spiritual bodies."

A calmness seems to come over Paul.

"The energy now, Christ holds the energy tight. I ask Him to create a pyramid of crystal clear light, one thousand feet high, above and below this room."

Paul says, "It's done."

"I ask Him to create a second pyramid of crystal clear light, two thousand feet high, above and below the first pyramid. In this second pyramid, there is an opening at the top, and I call for the guides and the angels to be there now. I want you to create a slight distortion around the second pyramid that indicates the feeling of betrayal. Tell me when that's done."

"It's done."

"I want you to call the essence of betrayal that's affecting the planet earth now, into the second pyramid and what does this energy look like?"

"Gray, black and swirling," Paul says.

"When it comes, it hits the pyramid, sees the truth and is sucked into the pyramid. It immediately moves upwards as the guides and the angels hold it and it transcends back to Source. And at that moment, specks of clear light go back out and touch every man, woman and child, the animals, the water, land and air, and brings them all back into balance."

Calmness comes over Paul.

"Now, I ask Jesus to hold that energy tight, the energy that is on your head. The pyramids will stay active until all this energy shifts. Now," Ken presses down with his hand on Paul's forehead, "how heavy has that been on you, Paul?"

"It's been tons, tons. It's this pressure on my eyes and body."

"We're going to release this off your eyes and body. On the count of three, we're going to take this back to God. Are you ready?"

"Yes, yes."

"One, two, three." And as Ken releases his hand from Paul's forehead, a wave moves through Paul and his face takes on a childlike softness. Then Ken says, "I want to speak to the entity inside you. Is it male or female?"

"Male."

"What's his name?"

"Peter."

"Where are you?"

"With Jesus. I denied Him, I turned away. I turned away. I couldn't look at Him any longer," Paul said, weeping softly. Tears were streaking down Paul's thin cheeks and the unbearable sadness of his cry tore at me, "He was suffering so . . . No one can imagine how He was suffering."

"Where are you?"

"In the dirt, the mud. I'm outside. Everyone is asleep."

"What color are you?"

"Red. Like blood."

"You look to the right, and what do you see?"

"Far off, a man in white. He's kneeling. He's praying."

"Do you recognize this man in white?"

"He is the Christ. Only the Christ can sweat blood. I hear Him breathing. It's raining. He's on his knees in the mud, His face in the mud."

The clouds have parted just enough for a moon to make its brief appearance. Its light wouldn't last long for already the storm clouds were threatening to obscure what light there was. The leaves of the trees rustled and struggled against the wind.

"I hear footsteps," Paul said, "I see torches. Someone is coming. They're shouting."

"Can you see these men who are shouting?"

"No, they're too far away. Wait, now I can see them. They're soldiers. They're coming to arrest Him. I know it. I reach for my sword. I must protect Him."

"Where are they now?"

"They're coming closer. I'm running and swinging my sword . . . Now, I'm in the garden, alone."

"What are you doing?"

"Trying to run. I have to go after Him. I have to help Him."

"Who do you have to help?"

"Jesus. They have taken Him away and I have to help."

"Yes."

"A soldier asks me if I'm one of His friends. No. I tell him no, I don't know Him." Paul is beginning to cry.

"A little boy is coming to me, asking what's wrong. Asking if I knew Him, He who the Romans had taken away. I said no. I said no, I don't know Him. I said no, don't you see?"

"Then what happened?"

"The child's father comes, asks the same question and again, I say no. No, I never knew the man."

"We're going to help to get you back to God, to where you can integrate and find balance and we can bring you back into oneness. This mental state is keeping Paul out of present time. Peter, what are you feeling now?"

"You know what I'm feeling."

"Paul, are you now in contact with that polarity or energy we call the Traitor?"

"Yes."

"We all feel we betrayed Jesus. And we all have our own ways of crying about it, getting mad about it, being afraid of it. Peter, were you there at the cross with Jesus?"

"They put a crown of thorns on His head to mock Him, He who was the Messiah who would lead His people out from under Roman rule, He who could not save Himself. But when they drove the first spike into His wrist, His head slammed back, forcing the thorns deep into His skull. And when they drove in the second spike, the thorns became part of His brain."

"That piece of Peter that is inside of you now, Paul, we are going to send it back to God, to find balance, and then we'll look at that past life in a moment."

Ken placed his hand on Paul's chest and gently pressed down with a firm gentle pressure.

"How heavy has that been on you?"

"Long ago it killed me."

"We're going to send that part back to God. Look up with your spiritual eyes, Paul. See the Light? Who comes for you?"

"He who I betrayed."

"Christ, hold Peter's hand, we're going to send him back to God. One, two, three." Ken released his hand from Paul's chest. Paul is becoming calmer and calmer.

"Now, I want you to go back in your mind, to that time, when you were with Jesus."

"I'm there."

"I want you to go back to when you were a child in that lifetime, I want you to go back to when you were a baby, I want you to go back to when you were with God. What did you come into that lifetime to learn?"

"I came to learn love."

"What did you experience?"

"I experienced betrayal."

"What are you creating in this lifetime?"

"Betrayal."

"How is that affecting the planet?"

"We are all betraying Him. We can't help ourselves. We think it's love."

"But we are all looking in our own tortured ways to love Him Paul, aren't we?"

"Yes. To love Him..."

"Can you let the betrayal go?"

"Yes."

Maybe it was a bolt of lightning that had suddenly filled the room, I don't know. An explanation might be that I was looking into the lightning just at the moment it struck, lighting up the entire room. Paul was screaming, "I can see. I can see."

I was only half listening to Ken and Paul. I could see the streets of Jerusalem. Passover was twelve hours away, and at home mother was already preparing for the feast. I hadn't wanted to leave home right then, with all the smells of food, melting candle wax, and wine, which on this day, I would be allowed to sip. I wanted to hear my father murmuring his hushed prayers beneath his white beard, for the sound of his voice comforted me, and would lull me to sleep, into one of those dream sleeps, where I'd imagine any world I wanted. In my dreams I'd be with my father, on his travels all over the world. He would come home and tell us about all the places he'd seen. He'd tell us about his trading and adventures, and I would imagine that I'd gone with him, that I too had seen everything. From Egypt, he'd brought the greatest prize. It was a crystal chalice, carved out of the purest quartz crystal. It was placed in the center of our house and was used only for the feast of the Passover.

Amidst my reverie, I thought I heard the word Golgotha - or garbage dump. I wondered what was so important about rushing to the garbage dump. I thought my father must be angry with me, and avoided his eyes. I didn't know what I had done wrong.

And then I could hear a voice, crying out, that no children were allowed, unless of course they were the prisoner's children. This time my father didn't respond. And then another image came to mind. A boat. No children on the boat. No children were to be allowed on the boat, two thousand years later in time. Then the images blurred together and I was left with a feeling of wonder at the power my father possessed, that no voice could stop us.

The heat of dusk was humid, a thick blood soaked heat like my hospital room after heart surgery many years later. My chest was tight from trying to breathe in the dust and felt as constricted as the bandages, pressing against my chest, had made me feel. My father told me to look. That I would remember this scene for the rest of my life. He was scaring me and I had started to cry and cough.

There are crowds of people. Voices jeering, whips cracking. I can't breathe. No air. My father had me in his arms. I could hear pieces of wood falling. I could hear yelling and commands being barked out and the words 'This is the place.' My father was speaking to me and telling me that my sister was alive because of the man they were about to crucify. And I remembered a day when my father and mother had been so sad, and my sister had been locked away from the rest of the family as if she was dead. And when she came out, there was much rejoicing and a male voice had said, 'People who do things like I have done will be crucified'.

The dust had obscured the sun. I still couldn't breathe and my chest hurt horribly. My father was telling me to breathe through my mouth but it didn't help. I was so afraid. All I wanted to do was run away and hide and all I could do was cling desperately to my father.

Then I turned my head and saw the face of my father clearly. It was Ken. He was my father. It was our family's tomb in which they placed the body of Christ. He was a merchant, a member in high standing of the Sanhedrin. Who else, but Joseph of Arimathæa, could have provided the tomb for the dead Christ? Who else but a rich merchant, a member of the Sanhedrin, could have arranged with the Roman soldiers to collect, in his crystal chalice, the blood of Christ? No Roman would have permitted anyone else to get that close to the prisoner.

Paul was saying something and my attention was called back to the scene before me.

"I'm seeing the ship, I'm seeing the ship," Paul was saying

166

"Who are you?" Ken asked.

"Paul. It's 1943, I'm on board."

"What's the name of the ship?"

"U.S.S. Eldridge."

"Are you in the Navy?"

"Yes. Ensign first class assigned to the U.S.S. Eldridge."

"Is it day time or night time?"

"Day. This guy has a kid. I told the asshole that a kid has no business being on a vessel during a maneuver. Oh, shit. Now the buzzing. The kid starts screaming, he's like four. He's got a death grip on this kid. He can't move."

"Why?"

"No one can move in the buzzing, in the fog."

"And the child he is holding? What about the child?"

"Crying. He's scared shitless."

"What's happening now, Ensign?"

"I've got to get to that kid."

Long pause. Paul turns over on his side, facing the back cloth buttons of the sofa and curls himself into a ball. And a very young child's voice is heard.

"It's okay, Paul," Ken soothed. "You're here with me and you're safe. Just watch what's happening, like it's a movie on TV Okay? Separate yourself and observe. What do you see?"

I was sitting in my chair. I was involuntarily opening my mouth to scream. How did he know? How did he know? I'm the child. I'm the one he had to get off the ship. If not, both of us were going to die.

It was Ken's voice. "Paul, you're safe. No one can harm you. You're watching what is going on, and it can't touch you, can't hurt you at all. You're safe."

Once again Paul's voice and posture was beginning to change, into the voice and bearing of a very old man.

"Who are you? Who is it I am speaking to now?" Ken asked, realizing that a new energy had entered the scene, through Paul.

"Chronos," an old man's voice rumbled. "I am Chronos."

"What reality do you exist on?"

"The past. The fiction we call the past. I am the past. I am history. I am all that ever happened on earth from time immemorial. I am history. I am what you cannot let go of, cannot understand. I am the lovers you never had. I am the dreams you had of them in bed, the beds they were never in, the love you only thought you felt but couldn't feel because of your fear. I am all you ever wanted to accomplish, the doors you never opened, the roads you never even saw but thought you were on, thought you were following but were too afraid to follow. And then you, the blind, gained access. A doorway into time, a window into eternity, was cut. By mistake, you happened upon other dimensions and were suddenly capable of traveling in the worlds of the past, bumbling about in the past, not knowing what you were doing or how it would affect the present and the future. Alter one speck of dust a million years ago and you have no idea what havoc you have reeked today. Because of me everything is unchanged. Everything is as it should be."

"And why have you come, Chronos?

"To do what no one else can do."

"Now the Past has to let go, give way to the present and the future. You're ready to go, aren't you Chronos? The present is all there is. The Past is a fiction, a memory."

And the room was quiet. And all I could hear was the rain falling outside.

The old energy, Chronos, laughed. "I am never over. Man refuses to let go of me. I am with him always. Man

168

knows not of the present. He only knows of the past. He clings to the past for he thinks I can save him, even as I trap him. Tell what the present is and I will tell you that the present has become the past before you know it. Before you can say a word the present is far into the past."

"You are done," Ken soothed, "Paul can now let go of the Past and you can release him. You said it yourself. You are a fiction, a story we tell about ourselves. I want you to look up and there's a special light that comes from your reality. Now, an aspect of yourself comes back and holds you and will take you home. Will you go?"

"Of course I will go. There is no present. So, I am gone already, aren't I?"

The thunder had reached its apex and lightening flashed through the windows as Paul lay there on the sofa, quietly gazing at the ceiling, his eyes wide open.

∞ **20** ∞

I knew I was running away, the same way I ran away from Mary, had always run from myself. I escaped into my room. I sat in my rocker and held onto the arms with all of my might. I looked at the white clock on the wall, at the second hand, as it clicked and jumped to the next dot. I was thinking of what I would have to pack, if I really wanted to get out of here, and the thought came to me that I would have to pack very little. I trusted them to send me the rest of my books, at a later date, so it wouldn't be that hard to call a taxi, late at night, when everyone was asleep, and once again become invisible.

As the hours passed into early morning, I found myself listening, hoping that I was the only one awake, praying that I still had the chance to get out of here sight unseen. Jon would always put me up for as many nights as I required, but what job would I be able to find with the condition of my heart the way it was now? How would I be able to live? Gradually, as the night passed, the only thought was to get out of here before anyone woke up, before I would have to speak to them. I ended up calling a taxi, which arrived an hour later and took me to the airport. I couldn't understand why I was so desperate to avoid speaking to anyone and having to explain what I was thinking and feeling.

What did it mean to believe in something, I wondered in the cab, on the way to the Austin airport. Would I really go through with getting on the plane? If the cab had passed a nursing home, or a home for the criminally insane, I would have gotten out and flung myself at their doors, pleading with them to take me in. Who was I now?

The escape itself was easy enough. I caught the first flight into Oakland, feeling that I had never left the Bay Area. I asked the cab driver to take me to Jon's apartment in Berkeley, but when I rang the doorbell, there was no answer. I walked to a nearby restaurant, knowing full well that except for my credit card, I had only change. I ordered coffee, then a sausage sandwich, which I left half uneaten. I had thought of getting drunk, but I didn't do that, so puzzled was I by everything that had happened to me. I thought of checking into a motel until Jon got home. He'd allow me to stay with him, until I could locate a place of my own. Then I thought of Mary's parents. They'd certainly allow me to spend the night, and I needed to see Mary, to tell her why I was running away a second time. But that would require money for a taxi, money I didn't have. Maybe there was such a thing as a cab that accepted Visa.

At the back of the restaurant a telephone yellow pages informed me that such a thing was well within the range of possibility, so I called a taxi and waited on the side walk. Leaning against a white stucco wall was a homeless man and woman. They had a small child. I gave the child the last cent I had. Then the taxi picked me up and dropped me off, twenty five minutes later, at Mary's parent's blue house on the corner.

When I pressed the door bell, I was positive that something was wrong with my heart and that if these feelings lasted another second, they would have to call an ambulance for me and all the melodrama would begin. I was more terrified than I could ever remember being. I closed my eyes and leaned against the wall so I wouldn't fall. I felt like I was held by a force field and was unable to move, unable to breath.

I pleaded for the fear to go away so that at least I could get inside the house. Maybe Mary wasn't there. Maybe Ken had called her after Paul's transformation and she was back in Texas, home of the mad men. I pressed the door bell a second time.

I thought I could hear voices from inside and then her father was opening the door and saying, "Daniel. What a surprise," and reaching out to shake my hand, just as Ken had done when he and Mary had returned home from Europe, and I had been in a similar daze or trance, on the other side of a Texas door.

Once I gripped his hand, and saw the warmth, the compassion in his eyes, I was suddenly feeling better and walked into the front hallway almost as if I was a normal human being. I could hear Mary and her mother in the kitchen. The TV was turned on. They were listening to Phil Donohue and Bob was saying, "Guess who's here?"

I slipped into the guest bathroom and stood facing myself in the mirror. The man in the mirror didn't look as if he had a heart problem at all. I wondered why he should appear so well while I felt so sick. I took a breath. I was standing up straight, I was breathing deeply. I was no longer dizzy. Maybe I was that person in the mirror. I splashed my face with cold water and reached for a hand towel. For an instant I thought I saw someone in white standing behind me, but when I turned no one was there.

"Danny," I heard Mary call, just as she'd done in the old days when we were married, and I had just returned from a day's worth of writing, the days when the heart wasn't the problem. There had been days like that, hadn't there?

I walked into the brightly lit dining room, the dining table littered with piles of unopened mail, canceled checks, and books from book clubs that hadn't as yet been opened, just like it always had been. "Hello," I called and Mary rushed into the dining room to greet me.

"Danny, is that you?" Mary's mother called as Mary lead me, by the hand, into the kitchen. There sat Mary's mother, Bea, smoking a cigarette, and smiling broadly in greeting. She was one of my favorite people, wise and beautiful, and I felt better just seeing her again. She reached out for a hug and said, "Sit down. Sit down. Danny, you look wonderful. I've missed you."

There were the same old stools by the kitchen counter and a little, black color TV sat by the window with Phil Donohue, in the audience, talking to a lady.

I perched myself on a stool and taking a few much needed deep breaths, said, "I've decided ..."

"Ken called me. I've been expecting you," Mary said. She went to the stove and quickly stirred a large pot, keeping her eyes glued to mine the whole time.

"Danny, tell me, how have you been doing?" Bea said, waving the cigarette smoke away as if it was a bothersome fly. A New York Times crossword puzzle lay at her elbow, a yellow very dilapidated crossword puzzle dictionary close by, her glasses and a ball point pen on top of it.

"He's fine now," Mary said from the stove. "When he arrived in Texas he looked like death." She stopped stirring. "How's Paul?"

"Whatever Ken did, it worked. Paul can see again," I said. "Maybe his blindness was emotional, or maybe Ken worked a miracle."

"Mom?" Mary asked, "Would you finish the stew? Daniel and I have to talk." Without waiting for her mother to answer, she grabbed my arm and led me out of the kitchen and up the hallway, to the stairs leading to an extra bedroom used mainly for storage.

"I don't want to upset my parents," she said on the way up the stairs. "I know this must be hard for you. So, tell me how you're doing with all this."

She moved by the two sinks lit up by large milky glass bulbs above the mirror to where the bed had been. Now there was only boxes of books and furniture piled everywhere. There were two brown chairs in which we could sit down, if a lamp with a base in the shape of a peasant woman carrying milk, was moved from one of them.

As Mary sat and turned to me, she sighed deeply and said, "I'm okay now. I'm done crying. I knew Ken's work could be dangerous, but Polarity's death was such a shock. He meant so much to me and we had so little time together. He was just a puppy."

She sat looking around the bedroom she had grown up in. Then she looked intently at me. "We haven't really had a chance to talk. Did you know that?"

I said I knew that. I told her Texas had gotten off on a questionable footing for me. "It must be the heat."

She stared at me. "You're running away again," said she. "I can always tell when Danny is in his running away mode. After all, I'm something of an expert." She waited and when I said nothing she went on. "If you don't agree with Ken, just tell him. I mean, he isn't forcing you to believe what he believes, is he?"

"No," I said, "he isn't doing that. It's me that's doing it, but I don't even know what it is. For nearly fifty years I've lived my life one way, and in Texas, that way of living entirely broke down and suddenly I no longer knew what was happening. Like now, I thought you'd still be crying over Polarity's death, but here you are with your parents, cooking stew."

"Polarity has gone from being just a companion to being everything, everything I think about, everything I feel." The tears had started to her eyes. "Yes, I miss him because he's no longer with me physically, but not so much because, you see, he's now always with me. He's become the air I breathe." She lowered her head and stared into her lap. "You said Paul can see again. Tell me what happened after I left."

I tried in my own clumsy way to describe the events that had taken place, the way Ken had gone about working with Paul, and the experience I had, sitting in my chair, watching the process. I told her how the motif of the 'eye' dominated all Ken's stories. "Paul and I were seeing the same images, telling the same stories."

"Do you want to understand what happened?" she asked.

I tried to think of what to say. Mary allowed the silence to stretch out and then said, "Ken is, I mean was, your father in a past life."

I looked at her. "You know?"

She looked away. "Ken figured it out shortly after he met me. I told him all about you and he knew. That's why he made the offer for you to come to Texas."

"Do you believe all this father/son business."

"You were there," she said, "I wasn't. All that is important is what you, Daniel, believe and understand. At some point, you will know what is true for you."

"The news is on, Daniel," Bob called from downstairs. "There was a big storm in Texas. Come down and watch."

"Be right there," Mary called and headed for the stairs.

I called after her to wait, but soon we were seated downstairs, Mary lying on the floor, watching the resulting floods throughout the Hays County area. Men in boats were rescuing those caught on the roofs of houses and I was sitting there thinking that a game was being played and I didn't know the rules. Jon had been right.

Several times I tried to suggest to Mary that we should talk but she continued to lie on the floor, half snoozing and watching the news.

Finally, I demanded that she get up and I told her father that his daughter and I had something extremely important to discuss. Bob nudged Mary and she quickly dashed into the kitchen to see how dinner was coming. Then we slowly made our way back upstairs to the bedroom where we could talk. Once again we were seated in those two chairs and I didn't know what to say.

"And you, Mary. Were you just a gate into another dimension?"

Her face had lost its color. A long silence followed.

I said, "I don't think I've learned much by being in Texas. I realize Ken tried and I'm grateful but I need things to make more sense." I waited, but got no response and so added earnestly, "I wish I could believe in these stories, in my dreams, but I know that certain stories, even though I'd like to believe in them, are nothing but wishful thinking."

"Doesn't it make sense that on the day we first met ..."

"Go on, finish," I said.

"That you had lived through a number of lives, gone through many generations of time and maybe, somehow, you did it in a matter of seconds?" She caught herself. "No, I guess that doesn't make any sense. Who would that make sense to? Only someone like Paul, who's been declared officially nuts. Your uncle was trying to save you on the ship, but you interpreted it as though he was abandoning you, throwing you away. I think the subconscious is the entire universe."

"What the hell does that mean?"

"Do you have any better description of that piece of our mind we don't use? That part that's not in time, that exists in dream time, that part of us which can't quite describe our experiences in terms of three dimensions. Yes, I think that what we call the subconscious, is the universe. Call it the collective unconscious, or call it what you will. What happens, Daniel, if that is true? The brain is that piece of tissue inside your skull, but what is the mind? The soul?"

"Bob, I think someone is at the door. Could you answer it, please," I heard Mary's mother call from downstairs. At the sound of her words, I caught my breath. I had began to say, 'It better not be Ken,' but after the first two words were out of my mouth, I could hear my voice as if it were in an echo chamber. And because I could hear it, it became increasingly difficult to finish the sentence. It was as if another voice had begun to speak, and what that voice was saying was a list of all the reasons why what I was trying to say was utter nonsense, and so I stopped in mid sentence.

"I'm on the phone," Mary's father called and then Mary was calling down the stairs that she was on her way to see who it was. She was already going down the steps before I could reformulate my reply.

I was staring at the windows which overlooked the city of Oakland and for an instant couldn't make sense of what I was seeing. I tried blinking my eyes and still could not recognize what I was seeing. The windows looked like square black holes dug into the wall, through which I would, once again, vanish. I thought for a moment that it must be the medication I was taking, but I had long since stopped the anti-depressants. I couldn't figure out what was happening to me and sat back in my chair deciding that it was simply an ugly residue of my Texas metaphysical madness, and that it would surely go away if I waited. I could hear Mary's glad voice of welcome and what I thought was the front door closing. I could hear Bea calling out "Who is it?" and "Tell them I can't come to the door." I kept staring at the black holes in the wall, which seemed to be getting denser, turning an even darker coal black. I could hear the television voices and recognized some game show. I tried to think through how I would tell Mary what was happening to me, but no sooner had an idea formed in my mind than the applause of the game show sounded. Then I heard Bob calling, "Is that you, Ed?" and more applause from the television set.

I am an agoraphobic, not a time traveler. If my uncle took me aboard that ship, I assure you, it was no big deal. He died in a Japanese concentration camp, not aboard an invisible ship. My grandmother spent years trying to get the Navy to tell her the truth about his death and why they could never retrieve his body. You see, as a little boy, I lost my hearing in one ear and that's why I heard the buzzing. My inner ear was to blame, not the cross and not some vanishing boat.

Lights and buzzers were going off. I tried to stand up, telling myself that it was only the television. The next thing I was waiting to be told was that Ken was here, had just flown in, and was about to inform me that I had never been to Texas in my life. I could hear Mary's voice, and now and then, she mentioned the word 'Daniel,' so I concluded, they were talking about me. Then there was no sound at all.

It seemed a voice had began speaking long before I saw anything, long before I saw the light at the window that was blinding me.

"Don't judge what you are going through," the light said.

I was speechless. I didn't like lights that talked to me. This was a sure sign I was losing it. Then the light was gone. And Ken was standing leaning against the window.

"How the hell did you do that?" I yelled at him.

"We have a long time to talk about that," he answered, as real as any three dimensional object can be real. "Daniel, appearing and disappearing are easy compared to what is really difficult in this life."

"Oh, and what is that? I don't think I want to know. How the hell did you do that?"

"Refrain from judgment, Daniel. That's hard. Miracles are easy. Judgments limit your experience to only what you know." He knelt beside my chair, just as he'd done with Paul on the sofa, as if I were now the client. "Do you know what else happens when you judge?"

I couldn't have answered had I wanted to.

"It means you divide the world into many little pieces, and then, to make sense of the many little pieces, you try to string them all together. That's what we call thinking. Stringing the little pieces all together. Refrain from categorizing everything into what you like and what you don't like, into good and bad, into polarities, and you remake the universe, your own universe. You can't live the same way, you cannot experience life the same way. Try it for five minutes, and you will first notice how many judgments you are unconsciously making, how many separations you are making, that you weren't aware of. You can think about bad and good as much as you will, but never prefer one over the other. Buddha called it the middle way, the way of detachment, the way of wisdom, because you don't refuse to look at something just because you don't like it, and would prefer to like something else. Then you will be able to look at both sides of every idea, and in doing that, you are no longer the same person. The higher dimensions are closed to us, because they frighten us. And they frighten us because we can't see them clearly, and why can't we see them clearly? Because we prefer to see only what we like or don't like. Don't stop thinking, just stop judging. And the world opens up."

I tried to look at him. I tried to understand what it was he was saying.

"From childhood we are taught to blind ourselves to any other possibilities, other dimensions, by our parents, by society, by what is considered culturally acceptable. When we are totally blinded to everything else, except the three dimensional world alone, we are called educated, grown up, sane and intelligent. Let go of it, Daniel. Just let go."

I was in the room and yet I was also standing far away, watching myself. Daniel was far off. Mary and Ken were far off.

It was as if the two of them were sitting at the end of a long tunnel where I would never be able to reach them. "Nothing is real any longer," I wanted to yell to them, but everyone was too far away to hear me.

The room was changing. It was as if the walls had given way to the blinding light of the sun. Where was everyone?

I could hear Ken's voice.

"Maybe all that matters is the reunion of father and son. Two people living both in and out of time. Two people trying to let go of both good and bad, sane and insane.

"And so," I managed to get out of my mouth, "if you're Joseph of Arimathæa, where's the Holy Grail? I was your son, tell me."

Ken was silent for a moment and then his gaze seemed to shift. He seemed to be looking off into the distance, but the distance was in his mind. Then he said, "It sits in the waters of Blue Lake. When the crystal was thrown into the water it became the water. The chalice became the water you drink, the water that houses the fish you eat, the rivers that sail mighty ships, the water children play in, women wash clothes in, the water that is used for the growing of grapes for wine, the wine priests elaborate at the Mass."

Downstairs, Bob was calling out that dinner was ready, and Mary was calling back that she'd forgotten the salad, and Ken was gazing out the upstairs bedroom window, at thousands of small fiery crystals which made up the night lights of the city of Oakland, in the state of California, in the United States of America, in the Northern Hemisphere, on the Planet Earth, the third planet from the sun, a star in the Milky Way, which is but a speck in the mind of God.

It was Ken's voice, it was my father's voice, I was hearing. And it wasn't a dream. Or, if it was a dream, it no longer mattered.

"Daniel..." he was saying, "Look straight ahead. What do you see?"

For the first time I looked straight ahead. And for the first time, I didn't turn away.

"And the seventh of the secret words?" I asked. "If Memory is the sixth word, what is the seventh?"

"Welcome home, Daniel," Ken said.

"You didn't answer my question. Ken. I have to know. Please. Help me."

"Yes, I'll help you."

"Then tell me?"

"Daniel, don't you remember? You knew all of this. Don't you remember? The seventh word encompasses everything, affirms even negation. This word is the yes to life as it is and forever will be. It is the yes to the past as it is and forever will be. It is the yes to the illusion of love, money, victory, and failure for they are gods and they are

181

your teachers. Separate, we are nothing but the beasts of the field. Separate, we are still riding the roller coaster of multitudinous polarities. But in that splendid union we are the highest confirmation, the yes to all life be it rich or poor, well or sick, weak or strong.

"No longer love or hate, but one. No longer mind or body, heaven or hell, ignorance or knowledge, but one. The seventh word is One. And in the grand union we hold the Holy Grail in the palms of our hands. The Holy Grail, that which we have looked for and now found, the Holy Grail is the many masks of the *One* God."

∞ **21** ∞

Bob was calling up from downstairs that the stew was ready. I didn't answer. Ken was standing there looking at me. Maybe I hadn't noticed it before or maybe it had just come into his hand, but he was holding the red rubber ball, Polarity's favorite. Before I could speak, Ken tossed me the ball. I caught it in one hand.

"Remember what Polarity taught us, Daniel. He taught us how to focus and he showed us how to play."

Holding the ball, I walked quickly down the white carpeted stairs not even stopping to shout into the kitchen that I wasn't hungry. Bob didn't hear me as I opened the front door and went out. It was an especially lovely night to take a walk, to be alone, to throw a ball up in the warm night air and catch it. I headed down hill on Coolidge Avenue, the decline assisting my speed and giving me the sensation of floating slightly above the pavement. It would probably be hot in Oakland tomorrow, not the same kind of heat as in Texas but in Texas one could find a goodly amount of air conditioning to escape the heat. Only when I was half way down the hill heading toward MacArthur Boulevard did I even ask myself where I was going or what I was going to do when I got there. And the moment I asked those questions, I felt perfectly satisfied to say to myself nothing at all. I was headed nowhere in particular and when I got there I was going to do nothing at all. The trees overhead blew in a cool breeze and I hoped that breeze would be with me when I walked back up the three block hill. Now it was assisting me down toward the busy boulevard, where buses and cars full of commuters were headed home for dinner.

If I walked straight ahead I would cross the boulevard where a stone Baptist church stood. Seated on the sidewalk leaning back against the stone exterior was an old homeless toothless gentleman wearing a sailor cap, his blue coat wrapped tightly up to his chin. I decided I would sit down beside him, not because I had anything to say to him, not even because I wanted his company, but merely due to the fact that I was interested in why he appeared to be cold on such a warm night. I sat down. He nodded to me as though he had met a friend, then he went back to his straight forward gaze out into the street where the cars and buses were passing.

"Fair thee well gentle sir?" he asked after we had sat there for a few moments. At first I must say I didn't know if he was talking to me. He might have been talking to one of the businessmen disembarking from the bus. But when no one but I paid any attention to him I could only assume he was speaking to me and I asked him to repeat the musical phrase he had uttered.

"Fair thee well gentle sir?" He repeated.

This time I heard the question mark at the end of the sentence.

"I fair well," I answered and heard in my voice a light musical gaiety I barely recognized. I was suddenly so happy I almost cried. Out of the side of my eye I saw him nod briskly and then continue his gaze. His wrinkled lips were almost over lapping each other in what might have been a smile for they had no teeth that could provide them with a structure, a form. His lack of teeth almost gave him a comical look and we both sat there relatively pleased with our exchange. I repeated his question again in my mind. He had asked, "Fair thee well gentle sir?" and I had answered, quite musically and truthfully, "I fair well."

And then for the first time in a long time it came to me, an illumination of sorts, something I had been looking for. It was so easy.

"I fair well," I said over and over to myself. "Not in spite of everything but rather because of what I have been through. I do fair well."

I got up and placed the red ball in his lap. For a long time he didn't seem to know it was there. Before he could thank me, I began to walk briskly down the well lit boulevard. Whenever the impulse hit me, I turned either to my right or left and called a chipper, "Fair thee well gentle people." I said it over and over again. Those I greeted must have thought I had lost my wits. The only difference between me and my new found toothless friend was that I hadn't needed to use the question mark at the end. No, the phrase was surely not a question. Maybe that was what I had learned. Maybe that was enlightenment. I started singing the line, giving it various melodies. I bellowed it out at the top of my lungs, walking down the crowded boulevard. I could for once open my eyes. I could for once sing out. I could even dance all the way back to the glorious hill country of Texas, my new home. All I had to do was say what I never would have dared to say before until now, this instant.

"Fair thee well gentle people. We are gods." The light turned green and I joined the crowed striding across the street. "We are the creators. We have eaten of the tree of knowledge of good and evil. We paid the price to be ONE with Him, in a state of Godness."

A woman at the street corner had just lost a quarter in the newspaper vending machine. "It's a very revolutionary notion I am trying to tell you." She rattled the steel box,

185

but finally gave up. "You who lost your quarter, you carrying the groceries to your house for dinner, you lovers all dressed up going to a movie, you the lost trying to find the right bus transfer in order to get home. Don't you remember? We were there that day in the Garden of Eden, all of us." Two cars blew their horns commanding the stragglers to move out of the crosswalk. "We spoke to each other, we cried with each other, we comforted each other. From the beginning of time, we were the lost leading the lost every step of the way back home."

A drunk was using his sports coat for a pillow on an empty bus stop bench on which he tried to sleep. I settled down on the bench beside him, me, who wouldn't have recognized himself. I almost wanted to wake him up and ask him what he had to teach me. Even if he had mumbled and drooled at me, I knew that his would be the voice of God.

I sighed deeply and stretched my arms out along the back of the bench. The late day sun still warmed my face. What a perfect day this had been. The world is exactly as it should be. My teachers are everywhere; my teachers are in everything. I am the guardian of the night. I am ready.

Epilogue

Are you afraid of death, poverty, sickness, or being alone for the rest of your life? Listen to me. I am going to propose a completely outrageous idea. Your greatest fear is your greatest strength.

I am not talking about your miniature golf course type of fears, the fears that come neatly wrapped and our friends can talk us out of if they persist. I am talking about the kind of fears that none of us talk about, none of us want to admit, the fears that lay hidden for a life time, affecting the smallest things we do, or try to do. Let us begin at the beginning.

How do you want to live this life? This is a deceptively simple question.

The odd and fantastic thing about that simple question, is that many of us do not think we have a choice. Most of us feel that we have been forced into a life style pre-ordained by where we were born, how we did in school, whether we made our beds and kept our rooms clean, whether we had nice mothers, whether our fathers were rich or not, or whether we were born black, white, red or yellow. We allow factors to determine how we live and who we call ourselves.

In other words, many of us think we are stuck. We are slowly suffocating in our perceptions of our everyday worlds. We have a job, a family, freeways, cars, swimming pools, divorces and love affairs, all of which go into making up our world. But in the end, we feel we have no real alternatives. Our lives, our very culture, has been served up to us on a stainless steel platter and we have no choice but to believe the tale, because it is the story everyone else believes, the story no one questions.

I have presented to you a far more radical notion. We just might have a choice, a choice of realities. You have the freedom to create new realities for yourself every minute, every moment of every day. You have gone to a lot of trouble to create those gut wrenching fears, so why not do something else with your creativity? A writer who could create your deepest fears on paper would be instantly called a genius providing horrible revelations of the human soul. Believe it or not your fears took some genius for you to develop through the years, so why not turn that same genius in another direction.

"Oh, if I could only be sure of something," I hear you say. If only you could cling to something definite, whether that be a god, or a mate, or a piece of art. But I laugh, as if uncertainty were the problem. The physical sciences are said to be in search of a certainty, of anything that can be believed in and not contradicted. The trouble is that the Holy Grail of certainty is harder to find today than it ever was. Increased scientific knowledge and technology has, if anything, increased our levels of uncertainty, not diminished them.

All truth comes at a steep price, because truth is subjective. Today, fiction is harder than ever to distinguish from fact. Fiction, in many cases, offers a truth more real than fact. I ask you, what if fiction and dream are as important a part of what is true as any fact you can name? What if your fantasies about how you want to live, were as true as your fears about how you are living? What if fantasies are the truest thing about you? What if Wallace Stevens was right when he said that your imagination brings you closest to God? What if the real world is far larger than you ever imagined? What if the problem isn't that you are limited, but rather we have a frightening time of it accepting that we, as individuals have no limitations?

In the world that I am describing, we have many choices. We can believe in nothing at all, for nothing can be known in any absolute sense, or we can open up our beliefs and believe in everything. We can open ourselves to believe in ourselves, in matter and anti-matter, in parallel universes and worm holes in time, or we can ignore these realities as good science fiction, but bad introspection, and pretend time is linear, and that only what we were taught in school is true. We can live like we want to live, or we can live like others want us to live. We can see the sunlight on the road and acknowledge it as a miracle, or maybe it's just another day like all the other days. But listen to me: this moment, as you are reading these words, will never come again. It will never be the same road you saw yesterday or the day before nor will it be the road you will see tomorrow. What if I were to tell you that the road you see today is infinite in its never ending possibilities?

Today, we know that at least ninety percent of our minds are unknown to us. We call that mystery the subconscious. We call that mystery a maze of archetypes, signs and symbols, mythic realities and legends, secrets, paradoxes, and the old and ancient nights of the soul. We call it a void, because it is unknown to us, yet it is us. We call it memory, fleeting recollections that flash in front of our eyes, ascend to the surface only on candle lit evenings or while walking under the moon. We can call the subconscious the home of dreams, a level of reality just as substantial as our ordinary, waking reality. We call it our 'Higher Self'. We can call it gods and goddesses. We can call it a gateway. A gateway to the eternal, to the bottomless pit of hell, or to the face of God. Open up the world to new levels of possibility and all your ghosts begin escaping from the closets of your deepest fears.

Fear, what a strange word. It comes in so many disguises. We use the word love when what we really mean is that we fear being alone. We use the word hate, when we are afraid of confronting ourselves and require another person to help take the blame, the responsibility. We use the word faith, when what we mean is that we are afraid of being left without knowing, without ever being sure again. We use the word ignorant, when we are afraid of being contradicted by those who might judge us. And we use the word patriotism when we are afraid that we, as a nation, are not the best and the brightest. Yes, fear is a strange, dazzling word. But there is a very special kind of courage and love hiding in what you fear. Fear is an onion. Peel away the skin and we begin our exploration into fear and hatred and love, into time and space, into what we know and don't know. We begin our exploration into the many masks of God.

www.KenPage.com

e-mail: ken@kenpage.com
1-800-809-1290 U.S. only
tel: 828-263-0330
fax: 828-268-9505
276 Watauga Village Drive, H222,
Boone, NC., USA 28607

Please contact the Institute for information on upcoming special events, private and remote phone sessions, weekend workshops, and Practitioner Training classes. We will be glad to answer your questions and send you information as well as a free audio tape of Ken discussing his work, philosophies and MCH™.

Available from the Institute:

BOOKS

The Traveler Ken Page And The Fallen Angel
Throughout history men, like King Arthur, have searched for the Holy Grail, wondering if the legend could be true and the Holy Grail is only waiting for rediscovery. Join Ken as he unravels one of the oldest secrets known to mankind, along with Daniel, his son from a past life.

ISBN 0-9649703-0-9 $11.95

The Traveler: Man's Search for Soul
This book goes into great detail about cellular imprints, emotional signatures, symbols, polarities, entity interference, thoughtforms, lost souls, health issues, karmic,

emotional and traumatic links to past lives, recognizing psychic attack, space connections, walk-ins, and clearing multidimensional blocks. Transcripts from client sessions which demonstrate Ken's healing process and its application in specific issues are included.

ISBN 0-9649703-2-5 $11.95

The Traveler And The End Of Time
The Secret Life of Ken Page
Contains dozens of fascinating and inspiring true stories, from the life of Ken Page. Starting with his humble beginnings as a seven year old entrepreneur, through his years as a millionaire businessman, to a dramatic series of miracles, triumphs, and tragedies that permitted him to do nothing else but what he is today: an internationally famous facilitator of healing.

ISBN 0-9649703-1-7 $11.95

MCH™ Philosophies and Applications
Basic Instruction Manual. Prerequisite to MCH™ 9-day Practitioner Training. $30.00

Advanced MCH™ Techniques
Advanced Instruction Manual for MCH™ 9-day Practitioner Training. $30.00

For the Love of August Blue - a novel
August Blue tells the story about an eccentric old man who believes that his mission on earth is to bring God to justice. On the way he becomes a national celebrity and effects the lives of all around them. Available in 1996

VIDEOS

Christ Consciousness Breathing Techniques,
   The Living Light Breath™ Video and Instructions
Two thousand years ago, a gate or portal was created and opened to all human consciousness by the Being known as Jesus of Nazareth, or Christ. The gate, which connects the body and the spirit, the realms above and the realms below, and the inner worlds with the outer worlds, was created and opened at the time of His death. The gate was specifically activated as Christ took His last physical breath, and moved into the Living Light Breath™. The Living Light Breath™ is a way to move into unity consciousness. $19.95

The Animal Healing and Clearing Video
Learn how to fully experience nature as well as how to clear and balance animals and pets. $19.95

An Introduction to Ken Page and Multidimensional
   Cellular Healing™ 1/2 hr. $5.95

AUDIO TAPES

An Introduction to Ken Page and Multidimensional
   Cellular Healing™
Ken discussing his work, philosophies and MCH™. free

Sound Vibration Tape
A 30-minute tape of Ken Page using sound to shift and clear cellular imprints. $9.95

PRIVATE AND REMOTE PHONE SESSIONS

MCH™ is a way to discover your own self truth. Its purpose is to assist you by integrating your whole being with your Higher Self. MCH™ looks for patterns that your subconscious mind is giving energy. Often times, no matter how much work we may have done to understand our mental, emotional, spiritual, and physical issues, there seems to be a missing piece which blocks our final resolution of these problems. As a result, we create patterns, over and over in our life, so that we may have yet another chance to gain the wisdom, understanding, and knowledge of our lessons. In addition, any fears or emotional residue we may be holding over a particular issue may throw further illusion over the problem, making it almost impossible to see "the bigger picture". MCH™ addresses ways the inner mind can assist in breaking through these self-made and limiting barriers.

MCH™ WORKSHOPS

THE TRAVELER AND THE LIVING LIGHT LOOP

A 12-hour program. All participants will be shown how to be centered and move into creatorship as well as full body awareness and beingness. Learn how to experience each moment throughout every cell in the body. Also taught will be the Living Light Breath™, which will allow you to bring Ascension into the personal experience of 'Inscension' as well as access higher dimensions. Some of the things you may experience in the workshop are:
• Learn how to stay in your space energetically, and have more energy • Find out why things are going faster, and

194

find quietness and calmness within that accelerated flow. • Learn Bi-Location Techniques • Learn Holographic Healing and Rejuvenation • Explore your mission and purpose for being on the planet at this time • Find out how to really be in the moment, instead of the past or the future • Discover a new way to lucid dream, and work out issues in the dream state • How to be in balance with both your inner male and female aspects • Find out how to dialogue in writing with your Higher Self, and get answers that you can trust • Learn how to connect with the dolphin and whale consciousness, and use it in your healing work • Get symbols that will help you to connect with information from your past, and from other realities • Receive three valuable and unique holograms that contain special information, both energetically, and visually • Learn to access a sacred, energetic gate created over 2,000 years ago • Have a chance to participate in a group-session with Ken, and understand what you have created in your past.

SHAMANISTIC HEALING
AND ANIMAL CLEARING

A 4-hour program in which all participants will be shown how to fully experience nature, as well as how to clear and balance their own animals or pets. Live horses, cats and dogs will be used in the class demonstrations.

THE MCH™ PRACTITIONER TRAINING

A NINE day, 80-hour experiential training that extensively expands the concepts and techniques of Multi-dimensional Cellular Healing™ to include the very latest knowledge and information. Students will observe complete client sessions, highlighting the latest MCH™ techniques. They will also have the opportunity to practice sessions of their own.

Topics covered in detail in the course may be, and are not limited to:

Psychic surgery
Dual regressions
Group regressions
Induction techniques
In-Utero Regressions
Rebirthing techniques
Holographic picturing
Addictions and phobias
Self clearing techniques
Unusual toning techniques
Remote session techniques
ET interference and implants
Drug, alcohol, and food abuse
Dehaunting of physical locations
Working with children and animals
Witchcraft, voodoo, curses and spells
Reconnection to place of personal origin
Handling of the ego, will, and client blocks
Recovery of oversoul fragments, soul theft, breakaways

Also included will be several different forms of Holographic Mind-Body Integration techniques which may be whole body breathing, Tai-Chi, Yoga, using the breath to travel, projecting 3D into other dimensions, and expanding empathic abilities.

Certification involves completion of MCH™ Practitioner Course, workbooks, and submission of video taped client sessions which demonstrate the participant's knowledge and expertise. Upon approval by staff members of completed course materials, students may reference themselves as an MCH™ Practitioner.